Hearts Communion

Marianne Evans

I0640473

Hearts Communion

COPYRIGHT 2011 by Marianne Evans

Cover Art by *Nicola Martinez*

White Rose Publishing, a division of Pelican Ventures, LLC
www.whiterosepublishing.com PO Box 1738 *Aztec, NM * 87410

White Rose Publishing Circle and Rosebud logo is a trademark of Pelican Ventures, LLC

Publishing History
First White Rose Edition, 2011
Print Edition ISBN 978-1-61116-086-4
Electronic Edition ISBN 978-1-61116-087-1
Published in the United States of America

Titles by Marianne Evans

Hearts Crossing
Hearts Surrender
Hearts Communion
Hearts Key (Coming Soon)

Dedication

This book is dedicated to the grace of God that is revealed through one simple, yet powerful gift: the gift of family.

Praise for Marianne Evans

Woodland Series:

Hearts Crossing is a Gayle Wilson Award of Excellence finalist for Best Novella of 2010 Southern Magic, the Birmingham Alabama Chapter of RWA

…a realistic look at Christians without being preachy or over-the-top. I know anyone who reads this book will love it. In fact, I hope there is a sequel. ~ 5-Hearts / Brenda Talley, The Romance Studio on *Hearts Crossing*

Both Daveny and Collin are wonderful characters who have a delightful relationship. I enjoyed the path to Collin's returning faith and the sweetness of Hearts Crossing. ~ 4.5 Books Top Pick / Silvermage, Night Owl Reviews on *Hearts Crossing*

Ms. Evans has once again delivered a book which I could not put down…I cannot wait for the rest of this series. If possible, it just got better than the first book. ~ 5 Hearts—Book of the Week, Brenda Talley, The Romance Studio on *Hearts Surrender*

Hearts Surrender is a satisfying, feel good romance that goes beyond mere happy endings…I can't wait for the next Woodland book to be published! ~ 5 Klovers— Recommended Read, Crystal, Kwips & Kritiques

1

Jeremy Edwards's cell phone came to life. A vibration sizzled against his hip, and as he unclipped his BlackBerry, the display screen lit up with an incoming text:

HELP! Ur nephew is raging with 101 fever. Can u pick him up from daycare n keep him 4 a while? Txt, don't call. Im in class. DESPERATE! APPRECIATE! C

Jeremy, JB to everyone who knew him best, re-read the missive from his brother, Collin. Collin's wife, Daveny, was out of town, pitching a corporate landscaping project in southern Ohio. Collin would be teaching his high school English class for another—Jeremy flicked his wrist and quick-checked his watch—two hours or so, depending on student demands.

So he stopped painting freshly installed drywall and stepped off the ladder, calling out to one of the crewmen at work on the task. "Greg, I'm gone for a couple hours. Tell Mindy I'll be back later tonight to install the dishwasher for her."

"Will do. See ya, JB."

Gotta love flexibility, Jeremy thought with honest gratitude. Leaving behind a living room buzzing with remodeling activity, he went to the kitchen of the modest, three-bedroom bungalow his construction company was helping to renovate. *Gratis*. There he grabbed his leather jacket from the spot where he had draped it over a chair at the dining table. After sliding it on, he texted his "yes" to Collin's request and hit the send button.

The project he currently spearheaded was part of an effort to give back to his hometown, especially as summer construction activity slowed down and a fiery Michigan autumn bent toward winter. That fact drove itself home as soon as Jeremy stepped out the back door of the kitchen and found himself buffeted by a stiff, biting wind. He stuffed his hands in his coat pockets, lowering his head as he jogged to his pickup truck.

He auto-started the vehicle, then his thoughts zeroed in on Jeffrey, his nearly three-year-old nephew. Jeremy grinned to himself. He was happy to help Collin. After all, Jeremy absolutely doted on his nephew—and everyone else in his family.

Climbing into the cab of his truck was a welcome relief from the elements. Before leaving, he pulled out his phone once again and performed a location search on Sunny Horizons Day Care Center. He had a vague idea of where the facility was located, but had never been there.

Navigation in place, he backed down the bumpy driveway of Mindy Nather's home, frowning at the cracks he saw in the asphalt.

"Needs work," he muttered, driving toward the business district of Saint Clair Shores. Meanwhile, he mentally mapped out crews, supplies and the time necessary to repair the driveway, tacking that aspect of the job onto the living room and dining room renovations, which were nearly complete. He used downtime at a stoplight to open up a pack of cashews and pour a few into his mouth.

Crunching the snack, he shook out some more and moved forward, following traffic to an area of the city that featured a number of stand-alone retail buildings. Behind them were neighborhoods full of nice homes, still-green grass and trees gone spindly and barren. JB munched on more cashews, chewing while he kept watch for the address of Jeffrey's daycare center. According to technology, he was getting close.

Sure enough, a minute or two later he spotted a wooden sign featuring a rainbow, a large sun full of rays, and the words *Sunny Horizons* painted in a variety of bold, primary colors. The moniker resided on a patch of grass in front of a well-maintained ranch-style home crafted of red brick that had been converted to commercial use.

Finishing up his get-me-through-to-a-late-dinner protein boost, Jeremy tossed the wrapper into a cup holder and turned into the parking lot. He brought the truck to a stop, thinking about his nephew. Poor Jeffrey. He'd take him straight home to Collin's place where the boy could rest up and recover in his own bed.

But what, exactly, should somebody give a sick two-year-old? How much of that liquid medicine stuff would Jeffrey need? While he considered, and made plans to call Collin on that count, JB walked past the window line of the facility and glanced inside

That's when his focus sharpened on the scene inside, and his footsteps came to an abrupt halt. A thought slipped into place with compelling impact: *What a gorgeous woman.* Long blonde hair fell forward in layers, framing a face that featured fair skin and expressive, baby-blue eyes. The straight, thick strands swung as she moved from place to place, spotting pre-school kids currently playing Twister, which caused his insides to spark. Jeans and an aqua colored sweater showed off a trim figure. She laughed easily, talking the kids through difficult moves and exclaiming when players tumbled and fell.

Quick as a blink he watched the lovely lady shift focus. She turned away from the Twister competition and whisked up one of the smaller toddlers who lingered shyly near her legs. Lovely Lady stepped into a clear space. Face alight with pleasure, she spun the toddler, who seemed to laugh and enjoy it just as much as her female charge.

In fact, the sensation was contagious. Jeremy smiled in response to the pair.

And I'm still riveted to the sidewalk. He silently chastised himself, performing a mental shake that jostled him back to the moment at hand. *Stay on point, JB! Jeffrey. Nephew. Sick kid in need of help.*

He approached the entryway and stepped inside. But rescue mission or not, he looked forward to meeting the woman.

2

Monica Kittelski moved with long-honed ease through a sea of bustling children. She automatically dodged bodies, an obstacle course of shoes, socks, toys, even spinner boards that were being used to aid in a raucous game of Twister. Unaffected by the stream of movement and cacophony, she made her way toward the man who had just entered the lobby.

Jeremy, she thought. *Jeremy Edwards. This must be Jeffrey's uncle.* Collin had called a few minutes ago saying his brother would be picking up the sick toddler.

The noise level was off the charts, but the racket didn't even make him blink. Stepping up, already extending her hand, she gave him an inner nod of respect for that fact. He accepted the gesture, and Monica found herself pleased by the calloused texture and warmth of his skin against hers.

"I'm Jeremy Edwards."

She squelched a grin. "And I'm impressed." He simply arched a brow and waited, looking around, likely for his nephew. "You haven't even cringed yet."

His focus zeroed in on her, and Monica was caught off-guard by the sly, playful curve of his lips— the sparkle in his eyes that ticked against her nerve endings. The lips were full and expressive. *Nice.* Her heart rate shot up, and a fluttery, tingling sensation washed through her body.

"No worries. I'm not *quite* a rookie."

Monica smiled, and so did he. "I've seen many a man stagger to their knees upon entering the bedlam of afternoon game time. I'm Monica Kittelski. The owner."

"Hello, Monica Kittelski. Daveny raves about you. And I won't be staggering any time soon. I'm used to kid chaos, so I guess I'm not just *any* man."

"Guess not," she sassed right back. "Thanks for getting here so quickly."

"Not a problem. Glad I could help out."

The playful spice of his personality dissolved into familial love and protection when he caught sight of little Jeffrey shuffling out of Monica's office, holding hands with Deborah Nielson, the co-owner and facility director.

Jeremy knelt to Jeffrey's level and opened his arms. "Come here, Chief."

It was those little things that told the full story here—the way Jeremy embraced Jeffrey—fevered kid or not—and the low, tender tone of voice.

Listless, Jeffrey snuffled, his chin trembling as he sank into his uncle's embrace. Jeremy lifted him up, and then turned his attention back to Monica. Residual tenderness lived in his eyes.

"Chief?" Monica asked, charmed by the nickname.

Jeremy nuzzled Jeffrey's plump, overly red cheek. Jeffrey seemed to fight tears, but a few spilled nonetheless, trailing against his skin. "Oh, man, buddy, you're on broil. Let's get you home." He peered up at Monica. "It's kind of a long story." Over Jeffrey's head, he delivered a lingering, steady look. "I'll have to tell you about it some time."

She could only hope. "I'd like that."

Jeremy made to leave, moving between the two plastic floor mats where kids currently called out and contorted like pretzels. He carefully stepped his way toward a low-slung wooden coat rack with small, square storage cubbies on top.

"Twister gives them the chance to learn colors, flexibility and left versus right. It's the best of all worlds." The teacher in Monica came to the fore as she led the way, or, maybe it was a touch of nervous chatter meant to deflect her intuitive reaction to the man. Monica pushed that idea aside for later consideration.

He glanced over his shoulder and their eyes tagged. "Best of all worlds is also that spinning session I watched you perform through the window a few minutes ago. Wish I'd've had more teachers like you growing up."

Monica's poised, smooth footsteps nearly ended in a tumble at his comment. Her heart actually stuttered.

"I'll just get his coat," Jeremy said, evidently unfazed by her startled silence and affected reaction.

"There's a plastic tub as well, right above it, with his afternoon snack." Monica glided a gentle hand against Jeffrey's back. The toddler took a deep, shaky breath and stuffed his thumb in his mouth, closing his eyes. "Poor pumpkin. He sure seems relieved to see you. He's been hit pretty hard. Here, don't disturb him. You're just taking him to the car." Monica pulled down his coat and went to work. "We'll tuck this around him nice and snug."

She lifted the hood up and over his head for additional protection. As she ministered, Jeremy's eyes went wide. "Houston? We have a problem."

Monica looked up at him. Boy, did he have great—no, make that *awesome*—dark brown eyes. "What's that?"

"I don't have a car seat. Oh, man. Guess I bragged too soon. I *am* a kid rookie."

More like a deer caught in the headlights, Monica thought with compassion. He started to look around a bit frantically, so she didn't wait long before coming to the rescue. "Know why they pay me the big bucks?"

He chuckled. "You know? I'd love to knock that one right out of the ballpark, but I'll refrain."

She rolled her eyes, but didn't restrain a grin. He was cute—in so many ways. "Because I'm prepared. Stay here. I'll be right back."

Monica went to her office and opened a spacious utility closet where she stored any number of odds and ends—among them a couple of ready-to-roll car seats. It paid to think ahead; in her line of business, stuff like this happened all the time. She lifted one and rejoined Jeremy, who looked at her as though she had transformed into Houdini himself.

"You just earned every word of praise Daveny ever spoke about you."

"Charmer." Monica scanned the activities taking place in the great room. Satisfied the kids were adequately supervised by Deborah and a trio of teachers, she gestured toward the exit. "I'll help you buckle it in. You just take care of the bambino."

"Thanks. Really."

Stepping outside, a brisk wind cut straight through her. Fall, she realized with chagrin, was giving way to winter without much of a fight. Jeremy unlocked his pickup with the keyless entry and auto-started the engine. Monica prepped the car seat. Fortunately he stood behind her, with Jeffrey snuggled in his arms, and he blocked the wind.

That is, until she straightened and turned around. A large chunk of hair skittered straight across her face. She reached up to slide it out of the way and immediately noticed she held Jeremy's full attention. The smoky heat of his gaze did delicious things to her insides; suddenly it didn't feel quite so cold anymore.

"All set," she said. "Just settle him in and drop the safety bar into place. It'll lock right up, and he should be good to go."

Jeremy didn't move right away. He gave a tiny, almost imperceptible shake of his head. "I'll bring this back tomorrow. Seriously, I owe you. I got the call from Collin and just took off. Didn't even think about how I'd get him home."

"No problem at all; that's what I keep this around for. I'll see you tomorrow."

Those deep-set, mahogany eyes fixed on her. When he smiled, it felt like the first rays of sun at daybreak. She took a deep breath and turned, hugging her arms to her midsection as he moved to leave. The wind blasted against her once again.

"Count on it, Monica." The chattering branches of nearby trees and tumbling leaf noise nearly drowned out his answer, but her name on his lips warmed her insides once more.

3

The next morning, Jeremy climbed into his truck and shut the door. Glancing to the right, he caught sight of the car seat that rode shotgun. He grinned like a fool, starting the engine and cranking the heat.

His timing, admittedly, was deliberate. At just after 10 AM, he wouldn't be missed at the project site for another hour or so. He had a bit of that precious autumn-into-winter flextime to spare. Meanwhile, the morning rush of parents dropping off their kids at Sunny Horizons would most likely have dwindled by now. He hoped he might be able to take advantage of some additional one-on-one time with Monica Kittelski when he returned her gear. The idea left him buoyed.

Sure enough, when he arrived, the semi-circle drive leading to the facility was empty, with a handful of cars lined up neatly in a lot to the rear. Jeremy parked and walked inside, car seat in tow. He was greeted promptly by the smiling staff member who had brought Jeffrey out of Monica's office yesterday. What was her name again…?

"Mr. Edwards, right?"

She offered her hand, and he shifted the car seat to accept the gesture. "Hi. Jeremy, please."

"Jeremy, I'm Deborah. Nice to meet you."

"Same here." Deborah was tall and slim, with

short, curly salt-and-pepper hair—maybe in her late forties. She seemed, by nature, a bubbly and warm-hearted woman. He couldn't help but return her positive energy, though as discreetly as possible, he searched for Monica.

"I'm sure Monica will appreciate the quick return. I'll let her know you're here."

"That'd be great. I'd like to thank her." He paused a beat. "Ah, for the loaner."

Was he just imagining Deborah's sly grin, those knowing eyes? She turned and walked away—headed to a doorway on the left of a short hallway. Moments later, out came Monica. Seeing her again hit him just as hard today as it had yesterday. Sunshine hair was held back by a brown clip, which naturally drew his eye to her slender neck, to the soft angles of her face. She entered the room, full of supple, alluring grace, and her energy instantly filled the space. Those clear, blue eyes brimmed with warmth. Jeremy took her in, and savored, enrapt.

"Jeremy. Hi."

"Hi, Monica." He indicated his delivery. "Where can I put this for you?"

She gestured in the direction of her office. "Right over here. Come on back."

He followed her.

"Are you in a hurry? Can I offer you a cup of coffee?"

An excuse to stay for a bit? You bet. "I'm in no rush. Coffee'd be nice."

"Least I can do since you returned the car seat so fast."

"Trust me—the speed of return is fear-induced."

"Oh? How's that?"

"Frankly, I couldn't stand the idea of someone getting stuck like I almost did. You really came to the rescue yesterday. I appreciate it."

"No thanks necessary. It's my pleasure."

Monica took the seat from his custody and settled it on the floor of the storage closet. That accomplished, she moved to a coffeemaker on the credenza behind her desk, but not before giving him a look that pushed heat and adrenaline through his heart. Once again, her sense of innate grace piqued his interest, and admiration. The moment between them lingered a bit. "How do you like your coffee?"

"Black is good. Thanks."

Jeremy settled on a small, brown leather couch positioned beneath the window. The window was closed in deference to a chilly autumn morning, but sunlight dappled the space of her office. As Monica poured two cups of coffee, he paid attention. Third finger, left hand, no ring. A vibration of satisfaction skimmed against his insides.

After passing him a rich-smelling mug, she sat down behind her desk. "So Jeffrey is still under the weather, I hear."

"Yeah. The fever broke last night, but Collin's not taking any chances. He took the day off to be home with him since Dav's still out of town."

While they talked, a myriad of items captured his attention, filling in bits and pieces about the woman before him. First came the framed photograph on her desk of Monica, surrounded by a group of people he assumed were her family. Next, there was a small, crystal bowl full of colorful jellybeans that rested on the corner of her desk. Nearby, her steaming mug declared: *Teaching: It ain't for sissies*. Jeremy nearly laughed aloud.

In juxtaposition, and curiously enough, a porcelain rendering of a ballerina, *en pointe*, claimed center stage of her credenza, just to the right of the coffee machine. The art piece drew his steady focus. It was intricate and compelling in its detail. On the wall behind the piece hung a framed print of a ballet scene, identified at the bottom as *The Dance Class* by Edgar Degas.

Hmm. So, family was important enough for memorializing, and dance was a reoccurring theme. Interesting. Monica tracked the direction of his gaze, turning in her chair to join his study of the classic painting.

"I got that at the Detroit Institute of Arts a few years back, when they had an exhibition of his work."

"I gather you're a fan of art and ballet?"

"You might say."

Jeremy's eyes narrowed in speculation at her evasive reply and the deflective posture she presented. Deflection didn't sit well with him when this pervasive longing to get to know her better reached in so far, and so deep. So he kept the thread moving. "The ballet part's not surprising to me."

"Oh? Why would that be?"

"Because I've been sitting here, watching you, and noticing the way you move." Her attention pinged to him, and froze. "You're effortless."

"That's very kind of you to say." Her fingertips, now resting against the handle of her mug, trembled just a tad. She looked down, her eyes veiled; the gesture struck him as charmingly shy.

"That's very kind of me to *mean*." He sipped from his mug to give her time to recover from being startled. And provoked. Color heightened her cheeks. Jeremy sipped deep, his lips curving against the edge of his mug.

Monica straightened, regrouping. "You know, at this point, I think turnabout is only fair play."

"Meaning?"

"Meaning you've figured out a few things about me. It's my turn to find out a few things about you."

Jeremy knew his answering look was wolfish—and teasing—but he couldn't help it. Inexplicably, he longed to nudge at her a bit. Push. "What would you like to know, Monica?"

She leaned back in her chair, her brows lifted in challenge. She was undeterred, and back to center. All Jeremy could think is: *Wow. This is fun.*

"You have the ability to be pretty flexible with the work schedule. What do you do, Jeremy Edwards?"

He relented, setting his mug aside for the moment. "First off, my friends call me JB. I own and run a construction company."

"Really. Wow."

"It's not any more of a 'wow' than what you've created right here." But, he did appreciate her sincerity. "I'm entering the slow season—which allows me a bit of freedom. In the spring and summer, I never would have been able to pull off what I did yesterday. Anything else?"

"Yep. What does the 'B' in JB stand for?"

"Blaise. My middle name."

No mask fell into place; no guard shaded her eyes. Intrigue and interest sparked to life. "That's a really great middle name."

"You think so?"

She nodded readily.

"I always hated it. Too stuffy."

"Not in the least, though I think JB fits you better."

"Yeah?"

"Yeah. It's catchy. More fun."

There is so *much potential here, so much more I'd love to explore.* But Jeremy wasn't inclined to move forward too quickly, and risk halting their forward progress, despite rampant chemistry. Besides, sadly, it was time to get to work. He stood, and Monica followed suit. "I've got a jobsite calling, so I'd better hit the road." He took note of her silence, the discreet way she studied him. She followed him to the exit. Before leaving, Jeremy faced her, itching to reach out, to touch her. "But, if you don't mind, I'll be seeing you again soon, Monica."

All she did was smile; the launch of it was slow and tempting. That alone gave Jeremy plenty of motivation to follow through.

∂∾∽∽

As if he needed motivation.

He secured wood molding along the ceiling line of Nather's living room, worked with installation crews who laid new flooring in the kitchen—a cream-colored, shiny ceramic—and he helped measure and cut floorboard trim. All the while his mind drifted. Thoughts of Monica filled him, a breeze of sorts— unseen, but powerful. He fielded calls and arranged details to line up a contract crew to repair the driveway, and she even invaded that simple task. She worked on him like an angel's call.

Late in the afternoon, his cell phone rang. He glanced at the caller ID display. Collin. "How's the Chief?" Jeremy greeted without preamble.

"On the mend, big time. In fact, and I say this with all the love I have for my son, I need a break, bro. One hour—two max. Basketball. Tonight. You in?"

"Seriously? I'd love to, but who's going to take care of—"

"Lemme head you off at the pass, Bro. Our beloved sister, Caroline, is sitting with Jeffrey." Collin snorted. "Trust me. She made it abundantly clear I owe her big time for a simple, yet mandatory, two hour window of sanity. Sisters. You know I love 'em."

JB kept from laughing, but it was a difficult proposition. Collin's tone was desperate. He seemed pretty frazzled by assuming the role of Mr. Mom, but that didn't keep Jeremy from wanting to needle his brother. "You're being a snark. About our sibling, no less."

"My *snark*, as you so *aptly* put it, is *justified*. Caroline's at the control switch, and she's lovin' it. I took Jeffrey out to get a hamburger. I figured a lunch together would be fun, since he felt great and had so much energy to spare. Big mistake. I swear, by the end of the meal we had the wait staff cringing and twitching with nerves because he was so rambunctious."

That only caused Jeremy to grin. "You're embellishing. To get your way. It's working, too."

"Four on four, JB," he growled. "The school gym's available tonight, and everyone else can make it. So, last chance and final answer before I move up the family ladder and ask Marty or Phil. You interested in a basketball sweat-fest?"

Jeremy's introspective, muddled mood perked up fast. He could use the time with Collin to perform additional reconnaissance on Monica. Jarred by the thought, Jeremy's brows pulled together, and his grip on the phone tightened. This was ridiculous. He was rapidly becoming obsessed. "Yeah, sure. I'm in. When?"

"Seven?"

"See you at the gym."

∂∞∂

The shoe-squeaks, basketball dribbling and game-chatter that took place in the middle of the Saint Clair High School gym vied for Jeremy's wavering focus. Distractions moved against him continuously in the form of soft, fluid images. And those images created a reoccurring theme—the face of a lovely, blonde-haired lady with luminous eyes.

In fact, he didn't even pay attention to—

The basketball smacked him right in the stomach, his fumbling catch completely out of character. Generally, he cleaned up the floorboards with these guys. Collin, his teammate who lobbed the pass, now called time out.

"Hey, bro," he said on approach, "here's some advice: How about putting some D in defense instead of distraction?"

During the pause, they went to their duffle bags and pulled out water bottles. Collin sat on the bleachers, and Jeremy followed suit.

Collin leaned on his knees and turned to his brother. "What's up with you tonight?"

Jeremy ignored the question. "What's the intel on Monica Kittelski?"

Collin looked at him with drawn brows, and he shrugged. In tandem, they downed some water before

Collin answered. "She's great at her job. Beyond that I don't know a whole lot. Why?"

Jeremy grinned.

Collin groaned. "No. No, no and no. Really?"

Jeremy tossed back another deep swig of water. He grinned again.

Collin openly stared.

"I enjoyed the rescue operation, and not just because it took care of the Chief, and not just because it left you owing me. By the way, boy are you ever racking up the family debts, pal."

"Like I'm afraid of *that* development. And?"

"And she's cute. She's sassy. I like her. Plus, she's got that whole Reese Witherspoon thing going on, which is enough to make any man—"

"Aw, JB! Back it up a second. You're talking like that about my son's daycare provider for heaven's sake. You get that, right?" But then the mano-a-mano teasing ended. Collin paused, seeming to test out the flavor of this conversation.

Jeremy waited. And waited.

"I can only add this." Collin rested his elbows on his knees and faced Jeremy directly. "She's pretty much married to Sunny Horizons. It's her baby in a way. Her world."

"I can relate."

"Yeah. You can. You created and built Edwards Construction from the ground up. You sweat the details, and the quality you provide, just like she does."

"Nothing wrong with that."

"Nope. Not a thing. Unless it's the *only* thing." Collin ended there, pointedly. "For her, it might be."

Jeremy studied his brother, pondering that

statement. "Can I take Jeffrey to daycare tomorrow?"

"Oh, man." Collin shook his head; a huge grin spread across his face. "You've got it bad, JB."

"Hey, maybe I'm just magnanimous. Maybe I just want to help out my brother while his wife's out of town. I'm awesome like that."

Collin snorted. "Yeah? Keep sellin' that line. You might get a taker."

"I'm serious about taking him in."

Collin paused. "Sure. If you want to." Another pause ticked past. "But Daveny comes back tomorrow night. What'll ya' do then, with no more Uncle-JB-to-the-rescue cards to play?"

Nonplussed, Jeremy lifted a shoulder and tossed his water bottle back into his duffle bag, reclaiming the basketball so they could resume the game. "I'm good at improvising, Coll. Always have been. I think on the fly."

Collin swiped the ball from his grasp. "Yeah? Then fly *this*." He heaved the ball—but this time, Jeremy snatched it out of the air like a pro and hit the court.

Head and heart now firmly engaged in the basketball game, Jeremy came alive. Team Edwards ended the night victorious by a score of twenty-one to fourteen.

4

Monica's evening ended at eight o'clock when little Tracey Michael bounded up to her at the conclusion of the weekly dance class that Monica taught for preschoolers at the Saint Clair Shores Community Center.

"Bye-bye, Miss Monica! See you next week!" Red curls bouncing, the effervescent four-year-old hugged Monica's legs and Monica chuckled, rubbing Tracey's back gently. The aspiring ballerina wore a pink one-piece, pink tights, and pink ballet slippers. Monica dressed much the same, except in a shade of pale blue.

"Your timing was awesome today. You were on the mark, honey. Keep up the great work, OK?"

Tracey beamed at the praise, and left Monica feeling like a million bucks.

Tracey skipped to her waiting mom, who waved goodbye to Monica as she linked hands with her daughter, and they left the building. Almost immediately, silence rode in.

Always the silence.

Monica sighed, but bullied her outlook into more positive territory.

After all, the kids might not be hers, but the life she crafted brought her close enough. No mistake, this could never be as fulfilling, never as important and satisfying as having her own children might have been, but this was close enough.

It had to be.

"Stop," she muttered sharply. Resolved, she pushed through the blackness, the longing, and forced herself forward. By now, this was standard operating procedure. She gathered her stereo and a white canvas carryall. Emblazoned on the front was the word *Dance*, crafted of carefully stitched, multi-colored sequins. The bag was a gift from a student she had taught years ago named Kim Chavis. Kim would probably be in 7th or 8th grade by now.

Sighing at the thought, Monica walked outside and took in a deep, satisfying breath. Fireplace smoke added zesty spice to the air; stars laced the ink-black sky above. Night wrapped around her, and she felt soothed.

Until she thought of Jeremy.

Monica stashed her dance class supplies in the trunk of her car and climbed in, starting the drive home. *What a great guy*, she thought. He was spirited, flirtatious, and handsome in that strong, provocative construction-worker way of his. His foundation? Family. That much she knew from her interactions with Daveny. The Edwards's family was large, and extremely close-knit.

Large.

Monica drove, and tried to ignore the bite of longing one small word could inspire when coupled with a second small word: *family.*

She pressed her lips together, opting to crank up the radio rather than continue that train of thought. Minutes later, she coasted her car to a stop in the driveway that led to her ranch-style home. She unlocked the trunk, smiling at the happy whoops and barking that came from inside.

"Coming, Toby," she said on a laugh, her arms full of gear once more. She fumbled a bit to unlock the back door then slipped inside. She barely had time to safely settle the stereo. Toby, her chocolate lab, was all over her, bounding and bouncing, sniffing and making all kinds of low, throaty noises while he circled her and reared up to gain attention.

"OK, OK! Let me get into the house, you goon!"

As if he cared. He head-butted, he licked, and Monica loved every second of his attention. Toby did a decent job of keeping that deafening silence, the sad bitterness, at bay. Dogs were great like that. All they needed, and wanted, was *you*.

Monica walked through her darkened house, flipping on lights as she went. She loved living here but, particularly at night, shadows crept in from all around. Emptiness filled the space like a haunting refrain. At that point, Toby's companionship and unconditional affection touched her heart, and kept her from wallowing.

Toby followed, still nudging and pushing. Monica knew the drill. A dog walk called. Immediately, in fact. So she didn't bother changing out of her dance ensemble. On dance nights, a neighbor walked Toby at lunchtime, but once she got home, late hour or not, Monica didn't mind the time spent in his company.

She remained bundled within a heavy, soft wool coat and grabbed Toby's leash. The instant he heard the jingle, he charged for the back door. Once he was next to her, he sat like a perfect, begging gentleman, ready and waiting.

Monica sneered at him, scratching his head, giving

his sides a firm, loving rub. "Yeah. Like I believe this attitude."

She latched him up, grabbed a plastic bag from her back-door stash and began their walk around the block of homes that made up her quiet, well-tended neighborhood.

The rhythm of walking gave her time to think and reason things through.

She was filled with longings. On a number of levels. Jeremy touched off a domino reaction in her heart and in her mind. Some of the energy generated from those falling chips elicited red flags. Danger warnings.

Strangely enough, despite their brief interactions, she couldn't form a retreat. She didn't want to. Getting to know Jeremy would be fun. Crisp air, steady motion and time to think helped her sort that one right out. Yep. There was absolutely no harm to be found in exploring a mutually pleasing relationship.

That is, if Jeremy followed through on that tempting promise from earlier in the day.

❧❧

Boy, did he.

The next morning Jeremy entered the facility, with a fully recovered Jeffrey in custody.

"Hey there, JB," she greeted.

He sidled her a look. The quirk of his lips let her know clearly he enjoyed her use of the nickname. He helped Jeffrey out of his coat. "Hey yourself, Jellybean."

She laughed, taken aback by the slightly audacious reply. "Wait a minute. Jellybean?"

Jeffrey tended to, JB reached inside the pocket of that same, supple, somewhat distressed leather jacket from yesterday and pulled out a bag of the candy. It was her very favorite. He stepped close and handed it over. "I noticed the supply on your desk yesterday. Figured you might enjoy a refill."

"Well you get big points for continuing to be an awfully good charmer. Jellybeans are my weakness, I admit it."

"Want to know what mine is?"

That playful spark, the absurdly tempting magnetism he displayed had her skin tingling, her tummy fluttering. "I shudder to think."

"Coffee, of course. Charm, by the way, is the blessing and the curse of the Irish, land of my ancestors."

"So's blarney," Monica retorted, which made Jeremy laugh deeply. "Feel free to have a seat in my office. I'll be right there after I help Deborah set up some art supplies for the kids."

"You sure I'm not keeping you?"

"Positive. Go on in. Make yourself comfortable."

Monica walked to a supply cabinet in the main room. She pulled out a stack of paper, and several plastic containers of water-based paints. She carried the supplies to a group of long tables and set them out, energized by the idea of spending some time with Jeremy before they had to move forward into the day. In passing, Deborah caught her eye and had no problem addressing Monica with a satisfied smirk, and an arched brow. Monica clucked her tongue and laid out materials so the kids could paint. But she blushed, too, muttering, "Oh, grow up."

"You first," Deborah retorted, off to start ushering

the pre-K kids into place.

Monica returned to her office, and, bless his heart, Jeremy had already poured them cups of coffee.

"So. You've already pegged me as the charming Irishman who's full of blarney, eh?"

"The evidence doesn't lie." She absorbed his interested gaze with a smooth smile that belied the way his attention worked through her system. "But, since I'm Polish, I'm bowing out of the whole ethic stereotype and mythology thing."

His brows went up. The two mugs remained suspended in his grip. "That does it."

"Does what?"

"Polish. Don't bow out quite yet. We have to go to Polonia. We *have* to."

"Since we've just met, and I highly doubt you're offering me a trip to my motherland, I can only assume you mean the restaurant. The one in Hamtramck." Eagerly he nodded. Monica didn't fight a laugh. "I'm Hamtramck born and raised. That place is an institution in my family."

"When's the last time you were there? What did you get?"

He was enthralled. He was salivating. He was the epitome of winsome appeal. Plus, there was something irresistible about watching a well-sculpted man doing battle with his stomach. For a precious moment, Monica savored having the upper hand, and she smirked at him. "Stop it. You're seriously about to drool."

"Yeah, I am. So what? Quit stalling and spill. What'd you have?"

"I had Polish smoked sausage and kraut." Then, she became just as distracted. In fact, she quickly warmed to the topic. "Oh! And I had that really great appetizer they serve—the cucumbers, onion and dill in sour cream. Do you know the one I mean?"

Jeremy was the one who smirked now. He set the mugs aside then stepped in close. He reached up and lightly stroked the corner of her mouth, and all things cool and temperate went up in smoke. "Careful. You're seriously about to drool."

Monica was lost. Suddenly she was assaulted by cravings—for food—for surcease to the hungers she felt—especially her hunger to build on this wild, heady connection to Jeremy Blaise Edwards...

"I think we have to go there. Together."

His statement left her silent, and blinking. "Ah."

"Get back to me on that. You're lost at the moment."

"Lost in a world of food." She longed to moisten her lips without being obvious about, well, moistening her lips. Attraction had completely taken over, but she shouldered that reaction to the side and met him in the middle of the field, saying, "I could be cajoled. I suppose, though, I should complete the tale by letting you know my last Polonia dining experience came about as the result of what turned into a monumentally unsuccessful blind date. How about you?"

Jeremy didn't move away by a single trace, not even a fraction of a millimeter. That fact left Monica swept through by a tantalizing, melting *pull*.

"I was there for a friend's birthday celebration. I had their beef and cheese pierogies. Like you, I indulged in that wickedly good cucumber dish. So, all things considered, I'm thinking we're more than compatible. In fact, I'd be about willing to bet tonight's friendly poker pot that our first date would be far from unsuccessful."

His smile lit her nerve endings and set them on fire. So she shored up her wiles. "Careful, there, hotshot. You're making some pretty strong assumptions. After all, I haven't even accepted yet."

He gave her a mischievous grin that made her shiver. "Maybe. But you will. I have faith." He sealed the deal by gliding his hand against hers, and taking hold. Teasing ended. He went serious, but just as intense, and ten times as provocative. "Are we on, Monica? You game?"

Oh yes. Yes, indeed. But she schooled her features into calm, unruffled lines. Just barely. "I guess that'd be fun. When?"

"Friday?"

She didn't even look at her calendar. In fact, her gaze didn't leave his. "Let me get you my address."

❧❧

It only took about ten seconds past Jeremy's departure. Monica clocked it on her wristwatch, stretching back in her chair as Deborah stormed the gate—or office threshold as it were.

"OK, day three with Adonis. I want information, Monica." To emphasize her point, she propped her hip against the corner of Monica's desk. She folded her arms and drum-tapped impatient fingers on her arms, clearly going nowhere until answers were delivered.

Demure and nonplussed, Monica simply looked up, and blinked prettily. "Information? About what? The uncle of a student? Nothing much to—"

"Oh, no. No dice. Kittelski, you fail to heed a pair of key points." Deborah lifted a finger. "First of all, I saw you when he came in the other day. Sparks flew like pyrotechnics around here." Up came finger number two. "Second of all, he couldn't wait to return that car seat and see you today." Then a third. "Now that I've witnessed round three today, I have but one observation. It's a good one, too."

Monica rolled her eyes, forcing herself to act bored. "Then by all means, don't keep me in suspense. I can hardly wait."

"You two are off the barometer."

Monica burst out laughing. "Barometer? What barometer?"

"The flirt and play barometer. Surely you've heard of it." She waggled her brows. "Seriously. You guys are completely off the scale. To kick things off there's the whole 'Jellybean' nickname thing. Then, you bat those obscenely thick lashes of yours and mention Polonia?" She shrugged widely. "Yeah, I heard that part of the conversation when I walked past the door. You'll *so* have a dinner date before this day is done."

Monica's throat went dry. Was this whole playful affection and discovery thing with Jeremy headed to those danger levels she sensed yesterday? Monica gulped, but gulping didn't help much. This was just harmless fun. Good-natured man and woman playfulness, with a date or two on the side.

Right?

"We've already...umm..." Monica was too taken aback by now to finish the sentence.

Deborah, however, whooped it up, then concluded for her: "You've already *made* a date, right?" Numb and wide-eyed, Monica could only nod. Deborah just rejoiced all the more, chortling. "Ha! *I win!*"

5

In a gesture that Monica found both protective and stimulating, Jeremy tucked his arm around her waist as they followed the hostess to a quiet, corner booth at Polonia. There he settled her comfortably before taking his seat.

Monica adjusted the fall of her dress, leaning back against the chair as she opened the wide, plastic menu and began to study the selections. Her mouth already watered.

Until…"Ew."

Jeremy lowered his own menu and looked at her in question. "Hmm?"

"Ew. I can't help it. I always react that way to the only two words on this menu that I just can't tolerate."

"Which are?"

She offered an exaggerated wince. "Blood sausage."

Jeremy laughed, and nodded. "I have to agree. Not one of my favorites, either. My brother Marty, on the other hand, absolutely loves it."

Monica cringed, but gave Jeremy a teasing wink, which, as she intended, made him smile. She resumed the task of narrowing her food choices, but Jeremy's gaze slid against her like a piece of silk. Behind the cover of her menu, Monica nearly sighed, flattered to be the center of this man's exclusive attention. His reactions made her glad she had opted for a decidedly feminine, flowing dress of deep green knit and simple, but tall, black leather heels. Yeah. She was on a mission to win, and maintain, his interest. No doubt about it.

But Jeremy kept pace with her easily. He possessed the kind of frame she loved best in a man—broad of shoulder, lean, and long of leg, strongly muscled, but not to excess. On top of it all, he wore a gray wool suit and vivid, burgundy tie with total flair.

He leaned close, closing the space between them. "You look fantastic, Monica. Absolutely fantastic. The ankle bracelet, in particular, is very eye-catching."

Monica nearly dropped her menu. He had noticed that small of a detail? Jeremy's voice was low and come-hither, but completely sincere as well. Granted, she had chosen her ensemble with care—right down to the drape of a few thin silver chains, matching earrings, and yes, even the thin, shimmering ankle bracelet that decorated her right leg. Still. Wow. "You make me very glad I chose the accessory."

"Good."

Her insides danced, but she ducked behind the menu, her pretense of dinner selection lasting just a few minutes longer. Soon their waitress checked in and they placed an appetizer order of pierogies to share. Monica added a glass of merlot to the mix; Jeremy chose a pint of beer. The selections arrived shortly thereafter.

He unfolded his dinner napkin and spread it across his lap. "I want your story. All of it. Then to now." A sense of quiet intensity wrapped around Monica's heart like velvet, almost protective enough to muffle the undercurrent of edginess his request stirred.

"Leave out nothing." But then he sipped from his drink and reconsidered. "Hang on. I take that back. Hairstyles, fashions and any kind of girl drama can be edited."

She forced a laugh. Despite the warm atmosphere, despite a call to relax her guard, alarm bells sounded. Sure, the warning chimes were just an undercurrent for the moment, but Jeremy's request triggered a tense internal circuit.

I want your story. Would he like it? She didn't think so, all things considered.

So, in motions that were well-practiced to the point of being instinctive, she executed a diversion. "Sorry. Yours comes first. You promised me a story of your own, remember?"

He paused for a few seconds, glanced down at the table. "Chief."

"Chief."

Jeremy nodded, albeit with trace levels of disquiet, and reservation. "OK. But I warn you now, it's not a happy story—"

"Not to worry. I have a few 'not happy stories' of my own. Still, I'd love for you to share it with me."

An intimate, testing silence fell between them before Jeremy nodded. "I only ask one thing in return." Monica leaned into the conversation at hand and urged him to continue with a look and a nod. Those eyes of his—eyes she could easily sink into—narrowed slightly. "Reciprocation."

She nearly flinched, but held her ground. She nodded once more. "Agreed."

Jeremy settled for that answer by softening, and relaxing once more. "I come from a family of eight— well—we *used* to be eight. Five boys, three girls. A total handful for my parents, but they somehow manage to see the best in us anyway."

"Gotta love parents. What happened to the eight?"

Jeremy flexed his jaw, deflected his eyes. "Eight became seven."

A sensation took over, akin to ice sliding down her spirit; the chill built, but then came a tender warmth. "I'm so sorry, Jeremy. How?"

He gathered a breath, blew it out. "We lost my oldest brother in the line of duty. He was an officer with the St. Clair Shores PD."

He paused there, and Monica drifted with the silence. It wasn't uncomfortable or awkward, but rather, a seek-and-find.

"You know," he continued quietly, looking at a spot beyond her, "there are things that happen in life that change you forever, no matter who, no matter what. Kind of like the gut-punch you never see coming. This was one of those moments for us. All of us were shocked and stunned when he was killed."

Sudden memories flashed through her mind—the recollection of news reports about a police sergeant who had been killed in the midst of a domestic dispute. "Lance Edwards—your brother was Lance Edwards."

Jeremy nodded.

"I was fairly new to The Shores at that point, which is probably why it stuck with me—I remember the media coverage."

"It hit my brother Collin the hardest, I think. You see, he was doing a ride-along that night, and he witnessed the whole thing. He even tried to help stop the perp—but Lance—well, obviously he didn't make it—and Collin wrestled with a lot of ghosts and negativity afterward."

Monica listened, enrapt.

"When he met Daveny, he found his way back—back to God, back to his faith—and he found the most incredible woman—a woman who's tailor-made for him."

Monica smiled at the romance of the words, the simple joy of them.

"When Jeffrey was born, I don't even remember quite how it happened, but the guys in our family started calling him Chief. We talked about it at Sunday dinner one time, asking ourselves why the nickname even began. That's when Collin piped in and put it in stone." Jeremy grinned, but a sadness lingered, etched around the corners of his mouth. "It's probably just family pride and all, but we decided, if Lance had survived, he'd've easily made police chief someday. Since Jeffrey's middle name is Lance, after our brother, we figured the nickname should stick."

Family love. Legacies. Children.

Monica's heart lurched. A sharp pang, accompanied by a lump that formed hard and fast in her throat, threatened to break her. She responded to an influx of emotion—emotion that had nothing to do with Jeremy's story, and everything to do with her own.

As ever, though, she pushed on, rebuking her feelings and shoving them away.

"I still remember every word of Collin's eulogy," Jeremy continued, unaware of her discomfort. "Collin is a born writer—a teacher of the language. He did a fantastic job. Me, I'm no wordsmith."

Safe ground. Internally Monica eased up a bit, feeling relieved. She slid into a shared moment of warm, meat-spiced air, soft dinner sounds, flickering candlelight and charming, checkered-cloth table linens that spoke not of ritzy elegance, but rather all things homey, comforting and *good*. The centering interlude helped.

"So how did *you* cope?"

Jeremy shrugged. "I swing hammers. I build. I get physical. What I went through with Lance is what brought me to where I am today. I work hard, I give thanks, and I give back by helping people in need." For a moment he toyed with the flatware next to his plate; the unsettled motion drew Monica's attention to the glimmer of soft candlelight against the toughness of silver. The parallel to Jeremy softened her heart, but shored her resolve to not let him in too fast—nor too deep. "He died in late autumn. My workload was slowing down for the season, and that's the last thing I needed at that point. So, I looked for opportunities to help some people in my community who needed construction assistance—fix-ups, repairs, that kind of thing. There was a lot I knew I could do, and I wanted to be busy. I wanted work. Work helped me think, and sort things through."

"So you volunteered your time with what? Community agencies and such?"

"I got more work than I could handle just by talking to my Pastor."

"Really." She took in yet another facet of his character and came away increasingly intrigued, and that lovely little pull kept coaxing her toward him. In fact, the strength of it increased exponentially. *Careful, Monica,* she thought in a building panic. *Proceed with extreme caution. This is enjoyable, but it can never, ever work. Not over the long haul. Not with everything you lack.* She cleared her throat, and found a smile. "Where do you attend services?"

"Woodland Church. I'm a lifelong member. I'm an usher, and actually just found myself appointed to the worship commission."

"Congratulations—I think that's wonderful. Your place of worship means a lot to you."

"God—Christ—means a lot to me," he amended. "Always has. Always will."

She didn't have much time to admire that conviction, that absolute faith, and recognize the empty void that loomed in her own heart. For in the passing of a heartbeat, his playful smile dawned, and it hit her hard, making her smile in turn, for no other reason than she simply had to respond to him. Add in those sparkling eyes, and she was swept away.

"Do you know what else?"

"What?"

"You, Jellybean, are one smooth customer."

"Well thanks for noticing, but where does that comment fit into our lovely dinner conversation? Not that I'm complaining, mind you—"

Jeremy laughed. "With an expert's precision you have absolutely and shamelessly allowed me to dominate this chat session."

"Chat session? Gee. I thought you and I were on a date."

He didn't allow that mischievous jab to gain traction. "C'mon. It's your turn. And then some. Can I have your story now?"

Monica lifted her glass and sipped—stalling, thinking, considering. Mostly she wondered: *How can I dodge the question? How can I dodge this man?*

The answer came in short order. She couldn't. She wasn't even sure she wanted to—baggage and all.

"If it helps any," he said, "I'll freely admit to the fact that you fascinate me. I'm not asking out of casual interest."

The intoxicating smile that accompanied that whammy left Monica dizzy, deliciously carried away. "What's behind this?" she whispered. "Don't you wonder about that a little, JB? Where's this...this *stuff* between us *coming* from?"

He leaned forward and distance evaporated. Firelight burnished the angles of his face. "Call it chemical. Call it magnetism. I don't know—but I'm on board. You fascinate me."

She let the words sink in and the flutters die down. She watched him across the small table, wrapped up by soothing, courting atmosphere and flirty sensation. The silence lingered, and lingered … but that was completely OK.

Jeremy softened, went tender. In his eyes alone, she found warm protection, safety and care. *So tempting,* she thought. *Such a call forward into every wish, every dream I've ever held.* "So. Jellybean. What about your story?"

On the inside, deep at her core, Monica began to shake, tremors working through her system in subtle, but unstoppable ripples. Soon, her hands would be trembling and he'd see much more than she cared to reveal. "Well. You already know I own and operate Sunny Horizons." Nerves got the better of her. She slid a lock of hair behind her ear, clearing her throat to steady her voice.

"Yeah. It's amazing. I give you credit. The place bustles like mad. Seems like a happy place, too. Can't be easy."

"Never," she agreed.

"Know what I wonder?"

"What's that?"

"What on Earth do you do when you have a headache?"

Monica's laugh bubbled.

"I'm not kidding! I can't imagine that level of activity, noise and the degree of focus you have to maintain. What happens when you're not functioning at one-hundred percent?"

"Believe me, I understand what you're getting at." She shrugged. "When you get hit, all you can do is survive. I suppose it helps that I pay attention to being healthy, and fit. I teach ballet once a week, so that keeps me in shape."

Jeremy gave a victorious nod. "I knew it. You're a dancer."

"I used to be. Especially in high school and college. I love it."

"OK, then, I have a stumper for you."

"What's that?"

"Tell me about your favorite moment on stage."

The question caused Monica to sit back, and ponder for a moment. He seemed so comfortable in his own skin that he inspired that same level of comfort from the people around him. It was a formidable attribute, especially when Monica considered how to continue avoiding the one, key topic that left her reeling with literal emptiness. Disconcerted by her natural guard and reserve being tipped upside-down, she was grateful when their waitress approached the table.

Jeremy welcomed their entrée of grilled sausage, steamed potatoes and the cucumber, dill and onion salad they both favored. They promptly dug in.

"I'd have to say it was when I competed in a state-wide competition for classic ballet my senior year of college. It was Christmas, and I danced to Beethoven's Ode to Joy. I took second, and never dreamed I'd get that far. It was amazing."

Jeremy stopped eating. He paused, fork in hand, and watched her with genuine admiration. "That's incredible." A momentary pause moved past, and he shook his head. "I'd love to see you dance."

How long had it been since a man made her blush? Ages. Jeremy inspired the reaction without breaking a sweat—mostly because his manner was so heartfelt. So *real*.

"So you teach." He had just finished a bite of food; he wiped his mouth and resettled his napkin. "That means you love dancing enough that you're still active. I think that's great."

Monica nodded, loving the mix of flavors that burst on her tongue when she crunched into a chilly, crisp cucumber, mixed with sour cream and a tangy slice of onion. "I teach pre-school ballet at the Saint Clair Shores Community Center. We have two recitals a year, one at Christmas and one in the spring. It keeps me in practice."

They ate for a bit in silence.

"So, kids. They're certainly center stage in your life." Jeremy winced. "Pardon the pun."

Monica laughed, but the sound came out false, and she knew it. Her hands clenched in reflex. She held her fork way too tightly and fought hard against the fear of turning him off, of losing his interest by virtue of being an incomplete woman. "Yes. I graduated from Central Michigan with a degree in child development. You might say it's my calling."

"Sounds to me like you'll make a great mother someday, Monica. Seriously."

Oh, dear Lord above, if only that could be true. A boulder rolled straight over her heart and pressed it down. Unwittingly, Jeremy had struck the bulls-eye.

Monica bit her lip so hard she could have sworn she tasted blood. She needed to call a halt to this conversation. Pronto. He had moved, swift and clean, past every single one of her defensive barriers. *How?* The one-word question raced through her mind.

She struggled, inside and out; this time she couldn't hide that fact. Somehow, Jeremy had worked his way inside chambers she had left barricaded. She tried to eat another forkful of their perfectly prepared meal, but the food tasted like sawdust now. She even tried to garner a casual, agreeing smile, but failed miserably.

"Hey…you OK?" Of course, he'd picked up on her mood; this man was both keen and caring.

"Sure I am. Yeah."

"Liar," he teased, smiling gently to temper that mild reproach. They eyed each other in momentary suspense. "I'm really sorry if I said something wrong, Monica."

She found her hand swallowed up by his; he held on, bringing their joined hands to rest on the tabletop. In an automatic way, he began to thumb-stroke her wrist in light, feathery strokes that made the flutters and tingles go crazy all over again. This man possessed just enough strength of heart, just enough appeal, to make her want to believe again. A night in his company left her wanting, desperately in fact, to leave fears and misgivings behind.

Almost…but not quite.

So Monica fell back on poise, and the veneer of a half-truth. "You didn't say anything wrong."

"Well, just for the record? The questions, the interest, aren't just superficial. This isn't causal first date stuff, Monica. I think I've made that clear. I like you. I already know I want this to be the first of many dinner dates. So have faith. Relax." He gave her hand a squeeze. "Don't be afraid."

Looking into his eyes, absorbing the satiny tenor of his voice, Monica allowed herself the luxury of sinking in and enjoying. She used her free hand to lift the goblet of ruby-red merlot and she took a deep sip.

Jeremy Edwards went to her head far more quickly, and efficiently—and with more real impact—than anything she had ever known, and she needed to find a way to move forward in a manner she could control and be comfortable with. After all, Jeremy was solid electricity to her, a heart-call she couldn't resist.

She definitely wanted more of him, so, she silently vowed to come up with a way to shore up her guard—to shield her own 'unhappy stories' and at the same time keep his interest and build on this budding—in fact flourishing—relationship.

6

Jeremy whistled a tune as he unlocked the front door of his townhome. He grabbed the day's mail, paging through a couple of bills and store ads. Then, he spied something a lot more interesting—a large, cream-colored vellum envelope with the return address of Grand Haven, Michigan. Rebecca Tomblin's wedding. Jeremy smiled to himself. His cousin. And she was a sweetheart. Last year had been a blockbuster for her: a move to the west side of the state, a meeting, courtship, and engagement to an up-and-coming executive at a pharmaceutical firm located in Grand Rapids. Now came the wedding, and it promised to be a blast.

After hanging up his coat, he tore into the envelope and pulled out the invitation. For the time being, he stood in the entryway. Just as he started to peruse the details of the event, his cell phone went off.

His smile only increased when he checked caller ID. "Hey, Mom." He could swear the woman had radar when it came to her kids.

"I miss you."

"Opening salvo delivered, and duly noted. PS? I miss you, too."

"Ahhh, but do you miss me enough to stop by the house so I can feed you? I'm sure you're starving."

"Me? Starving? Never."

His mom snorted. "OK. Where is my son, and what have you done with him?"

"You planning a get-together?" Jeremy walked into the kitchen and set the mail aside. Propping a hip against the long, main counter of green-and-white-veined marble, he opened the stainless fridge and pulled out some ground beef. For dinner, he'd throw a couple burgers on the stovetop grill and boil up some fresh frozen corn his sister-in-law, Stephanie, had given him a while back. One of the perks of being the only remaining bachelor in his family—he was pampered by the women.

"That's part of why I'm calling. Sunday dinner this weekend. Can you make it?"

The question caused wheels to spin in Jeremy's mind.

"I'm also wondering if you got the invite to Becky's wedding, yet."

The wheels clicked into position and began to hum in a smooth, promising motion. "Yeah, I can make it to dinner on Sunday, and yeah, I got the invitation just now. In fact, I'm looking at it as we speak." He picked it up once more. There were directions, an RSVP card and an information sheet on the venue for the reception, complete with photos.

"Small affair, at a gorgeous-looking Victorian-style bed and breakfast that's right on the shoreline of Lake Michigan. Should be lovely."

The descriptors were received, and then promptly discarded. Instead, he changed the subject. "Hey, Mom, can I bring a guest on Sunday?"

"Of course. At their own risk, naturally…"

Now it was Jeremy's turn to give a growling laugh. "Naturally. Edwards's clan gatherings do tend to be overwhelming."

"Anyone we know?"

"Sort of, yes. Monica Kittelski."

"She owns the daycare center that Jeffrey goes to."

Jeremy nodded. Another thing about Elise Edwards? Nothing slid past her notice when it came to her beloved grandkids. "That's the one." Dead silence greeted that confirmation. Jeremy could all but see the calculations taking place in a little cartoon bubble positioned right over his mom's head.

"Are Daveny and Collin aware of your...interest?"

"Collin is, so, by the de facto truth of pillow talk, I'm sure Daveny is aware, as well. I haven't heard about anyone leaping out of tall buildings, yet."

"Jeremy!"

"I'm just kidding, Mom."

"I think it'd be wonderful! If she's brave enough, we'd love to have her join the insanity."

Expectant warmth did a neat little slide through his body. "Great. I appreciate it."

"This is turning into a real party! Ken and Kiara are joining us as well."

Even better, Jeremy thought. The pastor of Woodland Church and his bride of almost two years were extended family to begin with. Secondary to that, introducing Monica to his family, and the importance of his church life, would continue forward motion in the relationship department—something Jeremy wanted to encourage.

"Sounds perfect. Thanks for letting me include her. My needling aside, Mom, she's a sweetheart. I'm enjoying getting to know her. I want you guys to meet her, too. I think the admiration society will definitely be mutual."

"Wow. This *must* be serious. You haven't wanted to include a significant other at a family meal in ages."

"Family dinners are reserved for only a few."

"In your case, *very* few. That makes me proud. You're not cavalier where your emotions are concerned. I think that's commendable. We need more JB's on the planet."

"That's a completely scary thought, Mom. Really." He pulled a batch of romaine lettuce from the vegetable crisper and set it on an inlayed cutting board. Next, he grabbed a knife. "Think about it. I'm the one who paid the most visits to the hospital growing up, and I probably pushed boundaries more than the rest."

"Perhaps, but character tells the tale, honey, and you've got it."

Jeremy squirmed as he began to dice up lettuce, but deep inside, the praise vindicated his decisions and way of life. Praise, or disappointment, from the parents was more than enough to lift him high, or chop him at the knees. "Thanks, Mom. My love to you and Dad. See you Sunday."

"Love you back, and I can't wait."

Jeremy ended the call, lost in thought for a bit while he completed his salad. His gaze settled upon the elegant invitation with its raised, scripted black lettering. He picked it up, tapping it against the palm of his hand. The inner envelope was addressed to Jeremy Edwards and guest. The wedding was six weeks away. Plenty of time to get a more definitive handle on this lightning strike of a situation with Monica.

Promptly her face came to life in his mind—and heart. There was that sassy, girl-power posture, her natural glow, those sparkling, warm blue eyes. And her smile—her smile alone packed enough power to send his pulse into overdrive.

I'm hooked, Jeremy thought, without a trace of chagrin. *I want to bring her to Sunday dinner and have her meet the family. I want to take her to Becky's wedding. I want to keep moving forward with her.*

His mom's comment was true—he enjoyed dating, but didn't allow many women into the sanctuary of his deepest heart, where his strongest emotions, his most precious beliefs, and his family, resided. The way he looked at it, some places in the soul were simply too precious to share in an arbitrary manner.

He whipped up dinner, ate, then toyed with a bit of romantic strategy while he unwound from the workday to the strains of ESPN. How best to ask Monica to a family dinner? The thought of dinner had his gaze tracking to the kitchen.

Hmm. Maybe that was it. Maybe he could test the waters by making her a dinner of his own.

≈∽

Rule one of courtship and male-female interaction: women love flowers. That in mind, Jeremy purchased a bouquet of white, pink-tipped roses. While the store clerk wrapped them in green tissue paper and boxed them perfectly, Jeremy penned a card.

Monica:

I hope you enjoy the enclosed. These flowers are meant to be an enticement to madness, chaos, and fun. Call me if you're at all intrigued.

JB

Directing delivery to Sunny Horizons, Jeremy could now do nothing but wait for her response.

During the next several hours, he lost himself in work. Easy enough, because today's assignment was a kitchen remodel in Grosse Pointe Woods that featured high-end materials, a tight deadline, and a high-maintenance client who lived in a massive, white brick number positioned along the banks of the Detroit River.

"Thanksgiving will be here before you know it! I'm opening my home to the entire family, and they're so particular. It's my first big holiday gathering, and all I see right now is chaos. It'll be complete, right? I have your word, right? You did promise—"

"The ceramic floor tiles will be installed today," JB assured her. "Once that's situated, we'll install the wall and base cabinets and the island, all of which arrived yesterday and are set to go. When that phase is completed, all that's left is placing the appliances. Those are shipping out the middle of next week, to conclude the project. We're operating on schedule, so I don't want you to worry." Calm and confident, Jeremy set about reassuring the nervous young wife of his client.

"My in-laws are lovely people, but they're so used to perfection, and the best of the best." Still obviously nervous, she looked around skeptically. "I never should have taken this on right now. I'll let everyone down."

Her slender form sagged a bit as she eyed tarps covered by dust, and workmen bustling through a large space that suddenly went small when equipment and supplies rolled in. Jeremy felt sympathy for this society darling. Obviously, she carried a heavy burden, and he wished he could find a way to help her see past outward appearances to the simple joy of hosting a family holiday celebration.

"I know remodels look messy, and we're at the point right now where you may feel like the dust will never settle, but we're in great shape, Mrs. Whittmore. We'll be done in plenty of time. You have my word."

Morning passed to afternoon. Despite pleasing progress on the remodel, Jeremy became increasingly edgy, waiting for a reply from Monica. When lunch break ended, he decided to check the delivery tracking information he had been given along with his order receipt. It was then that Monica's call came in.

"Hey, Jellybean," he teased. Her laughter tickled his senses, left him smiling, and relieved. *Connected.* "What's up?"

"What's up? Well, right now about two-dozen gorgeous looking, long-stemmed roses. In a vase. On my desk. And I've been presented with somewhat of a riddle."

"Really? Do tell. Perhaps I can help you solve it."

"Bet you can."

Jeremy grinned, strolling slowly into the welcome silence and privacy of a massive, perfectly appointed dining room.

"It seems," Monica continued, "I've been invited to—now how did your note put it? Madness, chaos and fun. No further elaboration, though."

"I wanted you to be tantalized."

"You've succeeded."

He pictured her, behind her desk, stretched back in her chair, looking out the window, perhaps, seeing the same rain pattern drumming against her windows as drummed against the large bay before him. He tracked the streaks of water that turned the pearly gray world outside to a wavering, shimmery shade of silver. "I want to cook you dinner tonight, if you're free. And I have a question to ask, about this weekend. But more on that, later."

"You're not going to give me the full scoop, are you, JB?"

"Nope. Not until you accept my dinner invitation."

"One of my many weaknesses as a human being is that I detest the task of cooking dinner every night. Therefore, I guess I better concede this match. I accept."

"Terrific. Come by whenever you're done at work." He gave her his address, and they concluded their call a short time later.

Returning to the kitchen, Jeremy looked at his watch. Anticipation curled through his body. Only three hours to go.

7

The front door to the daycare center came open, forcing Monica away from her present world of daydreams about Jeremy, and that breathtaking, unexpected delivery of roses. She heard the door buzz and left her office behind, coming upon a woman who looked around as though a bit lost.

"Hi," Monica greeted. "Can I help you?"

"I'm looking for Monica. Monica Kittelski."

"I'm Monica."

"Hi. I called earlier today about the possibility of enrolling my daughter at your daycare center."

Nodding with recognition, Monica stepped forward and extended her hand. "You must be Mrs. Carter."

The woman shook Monica's hand. "Yes."

"Come on back to my office and let's talk. It's a pleasure to meet you."

Business claimed her focus, but, once again, so did Jeremy. The image of him skimmed through her mind, and caused her lips to curve as she walked the narrow hallway with Caroline close behind. Monica pictured him, hard at work, in a gutted-out home, coordinating crews, swinging a hammer, getting physical in the way he had described so well at dinner. Once they entered the office, she closed the door and sat down at her desk, relegating Jeremy to the back of her mind. For now.

Mrs. Carter took the chair across from Monica, her posture hesitant. "Actually, I prefer Caroline Dempsey. I'm in the process of a name change. My husband and I are divorcing, and I'll be going by my maiden name. But, please, call me Caroline."

"Caroline Dempsey it is. I remember you saying you have a four-year-old."

Caroline visibly relaxed a bit, warming up as Monica recalled their conversation. "Her name is Jessica. She'll be five in a few months. She's been in daycare for a year now, but I need to change centers because I'm moving from Detroit. Until I find an apartment nearby, I'll be living with my parents here in Saint Clair Shores."

"So she's familiar with the routine of going to pre-school. That will make adjusting to a new center much easier, for both of you."

The comment seemed to set Caroline further at ease, and she smiled for the first time. "I hope so. I want to do everything I can for her. She's confused about all the conflict going on at home, and I'm not sure how she'll handle all the changes. I'm being even more cautious than usual about the facility I choose."

"No problem at all. We'll come back here and talk after I give you a tour of the school. If you'll follow me, I'll explain our pre-K programs and introduce you to our teachers."

Monica took Caroline through the main room. "Aside from being the lobby, this is also where we set up tables for group art projects, or floor games and such. As you can see, we have easels and paints, magazines and all kinds of cardboard and construction paper for the children to use."

Along the far side of the lobby, glass windows and doors lined the wall, revealing rooms that were sectioned off for each group of children—infants, toddlers, and preschoolers. Monica explained the workings of each class, then showed Caroline to the pre-school room where her daughter would spend the most time.

Once the door swung open, voices that had been muffled turned up full blast. Inside were about twenty kids, divided into groups for free play, reading and puzzle works. Four teachers provided supervision, moving from spot to spot when kids needed support, or questions came up.

As always, Monica's entrance was marked by shouts for attention. Two or three youngsters came up to her straight away and waited for a hug. She greeted them all, then picked up the last one in line, a shy newcomer named Joshua who beamed at her, but looked at Caroline in question.

"Hi, Josh." Monica gave him a squeeze and walked Caroline through the room, taking Joshua along on automatic. The only thought that crossed her mind beyond touring a prospect through her school was the idea of Jeremy, and kids, and how much family meant to him. By sheer dent of will, Monica refused to let the thought take root. JB had delivered roses and ready affection. *Fun and easy,* she told herself. *It's still just fun and easy. We'll keep it that way.* She refused to let sadness and trepidation diminish her pleasure.

Caroline looked through the windows of this classroom, into a wide open, large space, which once again, was full of kids. Monica laughed at Caroline's wide-eyed reaction, keying in on her guest once more.

"I call that the rumpus room. It's a real blessing on rainy days like this. As you can see, we have a small jungle gym, floor cushions for exercising, and foam balls to toss and kick around."

Letting Joshua run off to color, Monica picked up strewn toys and automatically stored them while Caroline looked around. The woman seemed pleased. "I like the art work."

She referred to a selection of drawings and paintings that covered a nearby wall. "We put paintings everywhere. My center is a showcase for budding artistic talent."

Caroline's eyes went distant, and troubled, as she watched the children play. "Everything here is so innocent. Carefree. That's what I want Jessica to have. I like your center, Miss Kittelski."

Absorbing Caroline's vibration of sadness stirred empathy, and Monica's encouraging smile. "It's Monica, please."

"Monica. I like it very much. Can I talk with you about some things in private?"

"Of course. Let's go back to my office and sit down."

When they returned, Caroline sat down while Monica moved to her side of the desk.

Caroline picked up a nearby paperclip and started to twist it nervously. "Monica," she began softly, not looking up from her fidgeting hands, "the most important thing in the world to me right now is knowing that my daughter will be well cared for and protected while I'm at work during the day."

"Protected?" The distinction took Monica by surprise, and her brows pulled together.

"Yes. Protected." Dropping the mangled

paperclip, Caroline finally looked at Monica directly. "I'm enduring a bitter divorce from my husband David, and I don't trust him. In fact, I wouldn't put it past him to try and take Jessica away from me. I have legal custody, but…well, especially lately, he can be volatile. If he got hold of her, he'd take her away, I just know it! I can't let that happen. I'm already at my wit's end. If he reentered the picture, I know I'd fall apart."

In a professional sense, Monica had faced this kind of situation before—a divorced parent, emotions taxed to the maximum, trying to look out for the best interests of their child. It left her heartsick on behalf of the entire wounded family—but most especially the innocent, unsuspecting child.

Leaning forward, Monica hastened to assure by carefully emphasizing her next words. "I have strict guidelines about who can and cannot take the children from my facility. When you enroll Jessica, you'll fill out a standard form that gives me the names of people you want Jessica to be released to should you be unable to pick her up for some reason. If they're not on the list, they're not allowed access."

"And that system works? I mean, I'm not trying to question you, or the rules you have in place, but I just—I need to be sure."

"Don't worry about asking tough questions. I understand. I'm very protective of the children I care for. I'm trusted to act on the parent's behalf during the day, and I take that fact very seriously. I have to." She reached across the desk and gave Caroline's arm a gentle, reassuring squeeze. "As we can't foresee every possible scenario, there are never guarantees, but we'll take good care of Jessica for you."

Caroline eased into a more relaxed posture.

"Thank you. I'd like to fill out the paperwork. I'd like her to start school here next week if possible."

Opening a desk drawer, Monica extracted a packet of enrollment forms and slid them toward Caroline, along with a pen. She debated for only a second or two before adding, "If you and Jessica are new to living in the Shores, I have a suggestion that might help her fit in and adjust even more."

"What's that?" Caroline looked up with interest, her pen now still.

"Wednesday evenings I teach youth dance classes at the Community Center. Jessica could begin in the pre-ballet class if you think she'd be interested. We're only a few weeks into the fall term, so she hasn't missed much."

"Dance." Approval marked her smile and sparkling eyes. "I'm sure she'd love it. You must really be dedicated to children. I admire your involvement with them."

Monica's gaze strayed to the stunning bouquet of roses. She breathed in the subtle, yet intoxicating aroma. In an instant, longing pervaded her spirit. *Kids. Jeremy.* She firmed her lips and blinked free of hope. Rather than elaborate on the thread of Caroline's conversation, Monica smiled, her hands going tense around a mug of cooled coffee from earlier. "Can I offer you something to drink? Some coffee or tea?"

"I'd love some tea, if it isn't much trouble. Thank you. And how do I go about signing her up for dance?"

Monica refreshed her mug and filled another with hot water for Caroline. Next to her jellybean bowl was a small tea caddy, which she opened and offered to Caroline for selection.

"The program is wonderful. It places no pressure

on the girls. They have a lot of fun learning and dancing for their friends and relatives. We have a recital in just a few months."

"A taste of show-biz. Jessica would love it, and she deserves the fun."

"I can get you those forms as well. They're right over here."

While Caroline continued to sign up for Sunny Horizons, Monica went to the black leather satchel she carried with her to work each day and sifted through its contents until she found a registration form for the Community Center dance program. "Here you go."

Caroline sighed, looking into Monica's eyes with heart-tugging gratitude. "A half-hour with you, and I feel like I just might get a handle on my life with Jessica after all."

The compliment provided a needed boost to Monica's outlook and helped her find an even center. "Thank you, Caroline. I'm looking forward to meeting your daughter."

8

"JB, your place is beautiful."

Taking Monica's coat and hanging it in the entryway closet, Jeremy absorbed the details of his home, seeing it through her eyes.

Granted, he injected a lot of TLC into the place, but that was half the fun. He loved open, airy spaces, so the cathedral ceilings, recessed lights and skylights suited him. He was also a fan of the polish and durability of ceramic, so the entryway and the nearby kitchen featured a smoky, salmon hue that offered up a visual of the warm welcome he carried internally.

Slow, but not shy, Monica moved forward, looking around with curiosity. He watched, and a mysterious emotion went to work in his heart. He found pleasure and a cozy sense of comfort at seeing her in his space, at watching her acclimate, and better yet, enjoying his home.

But Monica didn't fail him. She was also all about spunk, and sass. When she strolled into the living room, she tossed him an over-the-shoulder look that gave him a delicious heat rush. "You are *such* a guy," she muttered affectionately.

"Thanks for noticing."

"Seriously. The bigger the plasma, the better the man, right?"

"That's always been *my* mantra."

She laughed, taking note of little things. She paused by pictures of his family, slid her fingertips against fat candles in hurricane holders that were placed upon the mantle above a crackling fire in the fireplace. From a nearby coffee table, she picked up the remote and aimed it at the television screen. But she didn't activate it quite yet. "I'm making you a bet."

"Which is?"

"ESPN, ESPN 2 or, outside money riding on the NFL network. May I?"

"I'm up for the challenge. Go for it." Jeremy waited; in fact, he even arched a brow. Her eyes narrowed, revealing the fact that her confidence was wavering just a trace. He had set her a touch off balance. And he loved it.

She turned on the TV and was rewarded by...Fox News.

Monica sighed. She nodded in solemn defeat then turned to him. "I'm officially impressed."

"Like I told you when we met, I'm not just *any* man."

"Guess I should have paid better attention," she quipped, then turned off the TV and rejoined him.

"Actually, I did the whole man-versus-ESPN thing before turning in last night. Watched Fox before leaving for work this morning. So, to be fair, you almost had me busted."

"Your honesty is commendable. Regardless, you're a well-balanced individual. I like that about you."

That did it. Jeremy wrapped an arm around her waist and drew her in for a snug, warm hug that she returned eagerly. The moment ended with both of them sighing happily. As they parted, he leaned down, capturing her chin gently in his hand so he could prompt a subtle tilt to her head and kiss her cheek. He lingered a bit over their contact. Monica's eyes closed, he noticed, and her body softened. Welcomed.

"Are you hungry?"

"That's a loaded question." Her husky voice brought him back around, and made him realize the double meaning behind that question. They both burst out laughing.

"C'mon. Let's get cooking."

Monica gave his shoulder a shove. "Well, aren't *you* on a *roll* tonight?"

"That one was deliberate." He led her to the kitchen, guiding her by a touch to the small of her back. She was such a dynamo. He marveled over the fact, crediting her anew for the aspects of her personality that were so magnetic and appealing. In deference to her job with the kids, she wore dress slacks and comfortable, stylish blouses for the most part. Today's gray pants and softly draped, silk blouse of peach were both feminine and functional.

She happened to catch his perusal and looked at him with a surprising degree of shyness. "What?"

Jeremy touched her cheek in passing, making his way to the cabinet for cookware. "Nothing. Just thinking."

"About?"

"About the fact that I'm not the only one in this room who's a well-balanced individual." Monica looked down for a second, re-gathering herself, he imagined. Jeremy let her, and continued on. "Can I interest you in something to drink?"

"That'd be nice. Thanks. Today was kind of a tense one at work, and that weather's giving me a chill, too.

Do you happen to have any tea?"

"Absolutely. Name your herbal combo."

Monica giggled, and her blush slipped through his soul like the softest of caresses. "You crack me up."

"You're surprised. Again."

"Yep."

Jeremy clucked his tongue, and shook his head. "I beat you at the man versus TV game, and then you doubt my tea-making capabilities? I'm born and raised by an Irish mother who swears by a hot cup of tea." He pointed toward a nearby tea caddy. "I'll heat some water. Help yourself to whatever sounds good...and fill me in about that tough day at work."

For the next several minutes, Jeremy focused on Monica's description of her day, and, in particular, the episode with a new enrollee at Sunny Horizons. She kept specifics, like names and such, out of their conversation, but she appeared to be upset by the issues facing this single-working-mom. He retrieved a bistro mug from the cabinet above his built-in micro-wave and went to work preparing tea. She chose a version of green tea with jasmine.

When brewing finished, Monica accepted the offering with a grateful look. "You should have seen this woman, JB. She was desperate. She was completely at the end of her rope as a woman and mother contending with a bitter divorce. Furthermore, I have to say, I just don't get it." She watched as he began food preparations. "Can I help?"

"Sure." Jeremy handed her a wrapped package of ground beef and a frying pan. "This can be browned up, if you're sure you don't mind."

"Not at all." Monica lifted an apron from a nearby wall peg and slipped it on.

"So, what don't you get?"

She kicked on the stove heat, grabbed a spatula, and went to work. "I don't get people."

"People?"

"Splintered families, acrimonious divorces. It always tears me up inside to hear about kids caught in the middle of bad circumstances over which they have absolutely no control. It makes me angry. It's such a waste!" She blew out a stream of air, clearing her throat. She sipped from her tea, stirred the sizzling mix of meat and added some of the onion and garlic spices Jeremy offered. "And since I find myself on a soapbox, I'll end my venting session right there."

He watched, taking her in. "No need to do that. I don't mind your soapbox, or your venting." He paused. "You know—it sounds to me like she's trying hard to do the right thing. Maybe she just needs a hand. You've given her that."

"To a degree. It's like you volunteering, though. You always end up wishing you could do more, right?"

He loved her giving, tender heart. Propping a hip against the counter, he looked into her sparkling, beautiful blue eyes and went warm inside. "You bet. I wonder if she belongs to a church community that might help her out. If not, I'd be happy to pass along the name and number of my church's pastor. He's very keyed into the local organizations that lend assistance to people."

He watched as Monica steeled her spine, though she kept her voice neutral and kind when she replied. "That's really sweet. I'll keep it in mind, but I hardly know her at this point. I only know her side of a messy child custody situation. And her desperation. She wants good things for her daughter. I *so* understand that need, and desire. I gave her information about the dance classes I teach at the Community Center, and she's going to enroll her daughter, so that'll help, I think. No innocent child of four years old should *ever* be—" She groaned.

Jeremy glimpsed her discomfort, her realization that, once again, she was being awfully emphatic.

"Look. Never mind me. Let's give it a rest for now. I just want to relax, and enjoy being with you." She looked up into his eyes and smiled—truly smiled.

That made Jeremy feel better, but he kept Pastor Ken Lucerne in the back of his mind. He'd raise the topic once again, at a less vulnerable moment, and re-take Monica's temperature on the idea of connecting the two.

From there, meal creation continued. On the evening's menu—shepherd's pie. For the next half-hour or so, they danced around one another in the kitchen, and Jeremy enjoyed their natural, effortless timing. She stirred and stewed meat. He forked boiling potatoes to check for readiness. She sipped from her tea, then resettled the mug; feeling playful, he picked it up and tossed back a swallow of his own; he smiled when he set the mug back down and caught sight of her arched brow.

Reclaiming the mug, she met his gaze and took a calculated sip of her own. Jeremy watched, captivated. "Know what? Here's the thing."

"Oh, please don't keep me waiting, JB. I'm all about 'the thing.'" She offered a teasing grin, and oddly enough, it struck him that she even knew how to make a simple white apron look appealing. She wiped her hands on a nearby towel and continued to stir.

Jeremy drained potatoes and used a mixer to mash them.

"Do you know what this is—what we're doing here?"

"I guess I'd refer to it as dinner prep, with a side-order of tea commando."

He laughed, from deep in his chest, genuine in his enjoyment of her. Of *them*. "The thing is this: you and me. Now don't get freaked out or anything, but…" At that point, just to play torturer, Jeremy paused. He reclaimed her mug and lifted back a share. She waited, watching him. Whether she realized it or not, she was keenly interested. Aware. Intrigued.

Good.

"You officially owe me a refill." He nodded. "Tonight feels excellent. It's like you and I are a long-time couple. I like it. A lot."

Monica drained the meat, added it to the vegetable mix and stirred it well. Jeremy topped the ensemble with the mashed potatoes then put the metal baking tin in the oven. In unison, they began to tear lettuce into bite-sized pieces, but not before Jeremy caught wind of another subtle shift in her teasing spark, their light-hearted play. He prepared her a second cup of tea, and he realized that something akin to uncertainty creased her brow.

Testing a tad, he added further punch to his statement. "Additionally? My family's gonna go nuts for ya,' Jellybean. You're halfway there already, what with Dav and Collin already being fans."

"Yeah. Eventually." She cast him a quick, flirty glance, but it didn't reach beneath the surface. It didn't hit her eyes, or her heart. He recognized that fact immediately.

So, he sneaked up on her from behind and skimmed his arms around her waist, drawing her against him, snug and true. He nuzzled her neck and breathed deep—instantly assailed by the soft, tantalizing aroma of jasmine, lily, and *Monica*. She went lax, leaning against him. Her eyes fluttered closed.

"Actually, I want you to meet them. This weekend. Mom's assembling the whole motley crew for dinner. I want you to be part of it, if you're game."

Her breathing went shallow. He saw her pulse dance at her throat. "Really?"

"Yes. Does that work for you?"

"Are you sure that would be for the best? Do you really think that you, that I…I mean…I'm positive your family is great, and I'm excited to meet them and everything, but…I…"

She was speed talking. Charmed by that nervous reaction, Jeremy gave her a final squeeze and stepped away. "I'm sure. But more to the point of this conversation, are *you*?"

Monica untied her apron and slid it away. "I suppose—if they're brave enough to take me on, I'm sporting enough to return the favor."

Her voice was quiet. Her eyes were wide, deep and clear. She took hold of his arm, and stepped into him, a request for an embrace that Jeremy readily answered. Arms around one another, they stood in contented silence for a moment.

But layered just beneath that contentment he felt tension in her shoulders, in her arms and across the taut line of her back. She needed this physical gesture of support.

He attributed those undercurrents to the prospect

of meeting his large, exuberant family, and he let it go, hoping that's all there was to it.

9

Monica didn't get nervous about having dinner with Jeremy's family until she watched him pull up in front of her home. Only then did butterflies go wild in her stomach. Only then did her legs turn to rubber. Pushing those reactions into remission, she steeled her spine and welcomed him with deceptive calm.

"Be prepared for a spread," he warned once they were on the road. "My family does nothing halfway. Especially when it comes to Sunday dinner."

The trip took just minutes. When Jeremy entered a neighborhood of large, newer homes nestled upon rolling tracts of land, she gave him a look. "Success seems to be a genetic trait."

"Dad made a good life for us working for Ford. He didn't fall into this; he busted his back for it."

She studied his profile, feeling proud of the man at her side. "Like you."

Jeremy shrugged. "I suppose. Thing is, my folks give to their kids the way I want to give to my own kids someday. Not in things, and possessions, but in outlook, and character." He turned into the driveway of a gray brick, two-story home. There were already several cars lined up before his.

"So that's why you're so driven. To leave a legacy for your kids?"

"You bet. That, and to make use of the gifts I've been given. I figure that's my responsibility in this life. Know what I mean?"

He paused deliberately, waiting on her, she knew. But Monica couldn't speak. A choking silence forbade comment. That nasty, familiar boulder came back, landing once again at the dead center of her chest, crushing the hope in her heart. Giving up on further discussion, Jeremy leaned in to give her cheek a lingering kiss, then exited the vehicle. After opening her door, he helped her out. Monica trembled. *This exercise is going to be a piece of heaven—and hell.*

They walked through a lacey curtain of snowfall, approaching the front door. They didn't need to ring the bell. The door came open almost immediately by the hand of an attractive, bubbly woman in her mid-sixties. Jeremy quipped in a low voice, "Mom. She sensed our arrival, I swear. She has a kid-detection radar system that never fails."

"Here you are! Come in, come in!" Following her greeting, Jeremy's mom took custody of the coats they peeled off. Jeremy performed introductions and Monica took an appreciative sniff of the air. Already the aroma of slow-cooking meat, onions and pepper, filled the house.

"Something smells delicious," Monica said, following Elise's lead to the living room. There, seating was at a premium, especially for the guys, because the wall-mounted plasma screen flashed through sports reports and the Detroit Lions's pre-game show.

"We're having London broil, garlic potatoes, coleslaw and corn."

"Sounds wonderful," Monica replied, a sense of being overwhelmed sneaking over her.

"Ben, come say hello to Monica and JB."

Ben Edwards, the clan patriarch, rose from the couch, a twinkle in his eyes and laughter on his lips. "I tell you true, if it hasn't moved, Elise cooked it. She goes crazy for family get-togethers."

"Oh, please ignore him," Elise implored. "I simply enjoy gathering the troops. We're about ready to have some appetizers, but let's introduce you around first."

From there, the world of greetings and introductions became a whirlwind and a deluge. Front of the line was Collin Edwards, who gave Monica an understanding smile and a quick hug. "Daveny and Kiara are in the kitchen," he informed, "along with Caroline, Steph, Georgia and Kim." Monica felt her eyes go wide. This was a houseful. Especially when one factored in the numerous youngsters who presently dashed from room to room in a playful game of chase.

Family. It was such an enormous foundation for Jeremy—and such an empty, gaping hole in her life. Melancholy settled over Monica's spirit. She sank into herself, and hated the reaction, but all things considered, fighting inner demons became unavoidable. Following more introductions, they made their way to the kitchen. The Edwards's home was large and graciously appointed. Wood-trimmed stairwells, plush carpeting and crystal light sconces enhanced a formal, but not stuffy tone. Cathedral ceilings lent an airy sense of space and light to the atmosphere, and Monica couldn't help thinking of the similarities, the continuity, expressed in Jeremy's living space.

Jeremy kept hold of her hand the whole time, offering unspoken support as she was inundated by new names and faces. And charming, precocious kid after charming, precocious kid.

A kitchenette played host to the female members of the family as well as a few others. The sight of Daveny Edwards was a welcome delight. Fresh, vibrant and full of a joyful spirit, Daveny enfolded Monica in a tight hug of greeting, whispering in her ear, "You'll muddle through. Promise. The numbers aren't nearly as intimidating once you settle in."

Monica tried to laugh, but she felt hollow inside, especially when she noticed the way the nieces and nephews climbed all over Jeremy, showering him with hugs and hellos. She shifted focus, wanting diversion. That answer came in the form of an absolutely gorgeous woman who sat next to Daveny. This woman kept her eye on a man standing next to Elise; presently he helped prepare a tray of cheese, crackers and veggies.

"Monica Kittelski," Daveny said, "meet Kiara Lucerne. Kiara's my partner at Montgomery Landscaping."

They exchanged handshakes and smiles. Kiara gestured to the nearest empty chair. "Daveny has so many nice things to say about your day care center, Monica. I'd love to hear about it."

Monica watched Daveny stifle a grin and tuck a wave of chocolate-colored hair behind her ear. "Indeed she would," Daveny muttered.

Beneath the table, Monica felt a slight whoosh of air and motion. Judging by Daveny's sudden wince, it seemed Kiara performed a shin-kick to her friend beneath the table.

"Like I'm the only one with secrets," Kiara whispered. The two women shared a knowing look, then focused on Monica. "How long have you owned the facility?"

"For about five years now. It was in place before I purchased it, but the woman who owned it previously decided it was time to retire."

"Well I say God bless anyone who has the patience and stamina to educate and care for children the way you do, Monica." Up to their table stepped the tall, handsome man who'd helped Elise with food preparations. Dressed in a polo shirt and jeans, he radiated warmth and appeal. He sat and slid his hand against Kiara's shoulder in a gesture of quiet intimacy. *This must be the pastor,* Monica thought. *The one who heads the church Jeremy attends.*

The man offered his hand. "Hi, I'm Ken Lucerne."

"It's a pleasure to meet you. Jeremy's told me so many nice things about you. About *all* of you," she amended, taking in the table at large.

Conversations took off from there and Monica sat back, observing. Elise had silver hair, styled into a soft, neat bob around her chin. Dressed in black jeans and a bulky, cream-colored sweater, she looked far younger than she must be to have mothered all of JB's siblings.

Collin entered the kitchen and retrieved a couple of sodas from the refrigerator. He was, Monica now realized, so similar to his brothers in the eyes and face, and in physical stature, but the soft waves of lighter colored hair, almost blond in fact, and the green rather than brown eyes spoke strongly of his mother's heredity.

Then there were the kids. Of various ages and sizes, Monica quickly lost track. They clamored for attention, especially from Elise. Jeremy hiked one in on his back. Not surprisingly, both nephew and uncle were on the hunt for food. When he looked at Monica, Jeremy lowered the youngster. "Go see what Grandma's got stashed on the counter over there, Tommy. Looks like your fave—cheese and crackers."

Jeremy stepped up to Monica from behind, and she calmed instantly when he settled a hand on her shoulder. His other slid neatly beneath her hair, and he massaged her neck, kneading her skin with slow, gentle strokes. Heat bloomed at the center of her body and rose with shimmering intensity to the surface of her skin.

But the connection they shared didn't completely dispel an inner chill. She thought she had been prepared for this gathering. She was woefully mistaken; a sense of inadequacy played havoc against edgy nerves and refused her any semblance of peace.

"How many grandkids are there?" she asked Elise, who lowered the snack tray for Tommy's eager fingers as he danced from foot to foot. He snatched a snack, and off he ran.

"Say thank you to Grandma," came Jeremy's admonishment.

"Thank you, Grandma!" he called over his shoulder, not breaking stride.

Elise watched after her grandson with a happy expression on her face. "We have six grandchildren. And I'd take six more, thank you."

Elise set the tray on the table, and once again Kiara and Daveny shared a puzzling look. Ken ducked his gaze, reaching for the freshly positioned food offering in a manner that seemed more diversionary than anything else. An odd, unexpected sense of foreshadowing crept through her system. Out of her element, starting to tremble on the inside, Monica receded further and further to the background.

Chatter ebbed and flowed through the room, through the entire household, really. Jeremy took Monica on a brief tour of the place where he had grown up. At the conclusion, they met up with Tommy once again. This time, Tommy was trailed by Jeffrey, who hurtled into Monica and hugged her legs tight. "Miss Monica!"

She tried hard not to flinch. She tried hard not to stiffen. She tried hard not to back off when one of the nieces joined in as well, charging forward to join their little group. Tommy bounced up and down. "Uncle JB, come play a game with me and Katie."

"I pway! I pway! I wan' Miss Monica, too," little Jeffrey declared, not releasing his hold.

"She can come, too," Tommy appeased.

The trio of children waited expectantly. Jeremy looked at Monica. She wanted to offer the genuine smile for which he waited. She tried to nod in agreement. Instead, she froze. She longed for an escape hatch—a release from the pressure-cooker sensation that settled around her body and squeezed out every good emotion she should have been feeling right now. Kids and family were a huge equation in Jeremy's life. That didn't bode well for their future. Not from Monica's perspective.

Kid-play just wasn't in her right now.

"Tell you what, Uncle JB, you hit the game room. I'm going to visit the kitchen and see if Elise needs any help."

She ignored Jeffrey's disappointed expression, Jeremy's silent surprise. She turned fast toward the kitchen just in time to see Elise at the threshold of the family room. Jeremy's mom witnessed the exchange and watched in dark puzzlement.

"Actually, I'm all set," Elise said. "You and Jeremy should just relax and enjoy yourselves. Really, go along and have fun."

Monica pressed her lips together, looking away. Defeated on a number of levels, she nodded, pasted on a smile, and followed slowly after Jeremy and the kids. But she couldn't help noticing Elise's expression had gone sharper still. Speculative.

After the board game came a bracing, exuberant game of soccer in the backyard that teamed adults against the kids. Once again, Monica tried to step to the sidelines but Jeremy would have none of that. He brought her in full-bore until Monica was dashing across the lawn along with everyone else, chasing after the black and white striped Spaulding in family-friendly competition. Still, she caught the vibration of puzzlement escalating on behalf of both Jeremy and Elise.

The weather was cold, accented by an on-and-off sputtering of snowflakes, so it was a short match, designed to allow the kids to blow off a bit of cabin fever and build an appetite for dinner. Monica's attempts at play were halfhearted at best—until, at one point, little Jeffrey looked over at her from across the expanse of the backyard. He smiled greatly, and wiggled his fingers. A lump, inspired by longing, expanded in Monica's throat. Stinging, cold wind bit through her, so if anyone noticed that her eyes filled, she could blame it on anything but the ache in her heart. She blew Jeffrey a little kiss and wiggled her fingers right back.

After the match, Jeffrey dashed straight for her. "Miss Monica, you good! Fun, huh? I good, too!"

Monica was so wrapped up in the goings on of her heart, so troubled by thoughts of the family that bounded in and out of focus, she found herself at a loss when the youngster settled warmly against the side of her leg. Jeffrey looked up at her, eager and waiting. Monica realized he probably expected the comfort and familiarity of the way she treated him at Sunny Horizons.

There, in her own environment, she wouldn't hesitate to swing him into the air, or carry him along on her hip as she walked through the center. She could claim temporary possession when she was at Sunny Horizons. To coddle and "parent" him there was as natural as breathing.

But right now Monica was galaxies away from her carefully cultivated element. Jeffrey was centered within the heart of his family. *Jeremy's* family. At this moment, everything she longed for the most remained painfully out of reach, yet at the same time, it was on display before her like an explosion of glitter dust floating on the air—breathtakingly beautiful, yet impossible to claim as her own.

So, Monica couldn't muster much of a reaction to his arrival other than a wan smile. "I did see you play. You're outstanding. Are you having fun with all your cousins and aunts and uncles?"

"Mm-hmm. I like food."

Spoken like a true Edwards. Monica couldn't help melting just a trace; she even chuckled. "Me, too."

"Is it fun? Are you fun, like me?" He tilted his head. "You look sad."

Taken thoroughly aback, Monica opened her mouth, intending to answer, somehow. Words stalled. She looked at Jeffrey and her mind went blank. Early on in her career, Monica had learned absolutely nothing escaped the notice of a child. She should have remembered that axiom.

Jeffrey's brows pulled together until they puckered with curiosity. "Wanna pway again? I pway a game wif Uncle Marty." He pointed toward a nearby gathering. "You pway good games. C'mon!"

The youngster smiled; Monica ached. "No thank you, Jeffrey. I'm going to go back inside and warm up for a little bit."

He surrendered with a nod, but watched her in continuing bewilderment. "'Kay."

After Jeffrey scampered off, things progressed a bit more comfortably until dinner ended. Elsie went about taking meal-concluding coffee orders.

"Decaf, please," came Daveny's surprisingly chipper request.

Kiara spoke up, sounding equally cheerful. "Since misery loves company, I'll go for some decaf as well, Elise. If it's not too much trouble."

Jeremy rolled his eyes. "Oh, come on. Seriously? Decaf? After a dinner like this? You two need to learn how to drink coffee."

As realization dawned in Monica, the table at large shared a round of laughter at Jeremy's oblivious words. Elise, frozen in place, simply stood at the counter, a coffee pot suspended in her grip. She stared at the two women; she began to smile, and glow. Tears filled her eyes.

"Sorry to humiliate you, JB," Daveny said, "but I'm on decaf for at least the next six months."

"Hmm. More like five for me," Kiara chimed in.

Ken couldn't seem to resist. He slid the thick fall of Kiara's dark blonde hair over her shoulder and nuzzled her neck. He rested a protective hand against her abdomen.

Jeremy eyes widened as he finally caught the gist of their interplay. "We're pregnant?"

Daveny and Kiara cracked up, and the Edwards family erupted with congratulations and delighted, happy shouts. "We're pregnant," the women said in unison.

"I refer to it as an abundance of blessings," Ken concluded, keeping loving hold of his wife.

It took every ounce of willpower and grace Monica possessed to keep from running out of the room in tears. She only hoped the assemblage would blame her flushed cheeks and moist eyes on the news of the day and nothing else.

In truth, her heart was shattered.

అ∽ు

The congratulatory hubbub slowly died down. As quickly as tact and discretion allowed, Monica intended to head outside for a spell of cold, reviving air. Respite became paramount.

An abundance of blessings. Ken had put it so well.

But what about the other side of that coin? Monica wondered, ceding a mite to the devil's temptation. *What would the good pastor have to say about a* denial *of blessings? What about trampled hopes? What about a literal and figurative emptiness?*

Resentment pushed into her heart. Bitterness cut a deep line into her spirit and moved right in. Trying hard to outrun her feelings, Monica walked through the kitchen. A set of sliding glass doors led outside like a portal to salvation.

"Monica?"

She froze and winced at the summons that came to her from behind. Her hands trembled, but she steadied herself and turned toward Jeremy's mother, schooling agitation from her features as best she could. "Yes?" She forced a smile and bullied herself to be carefree and calm. The attempt failed abysmally, and she knew it.

"You seem…" Elise stumbled over her words. She frowned and lowered her gaze briefly. When she looked up again, it was plain to see she was fighting a battle against interfering and pushing at her son's girlfriend.

They were both walking on eggshells, Monica realized.

"You've seemed troubled throughout the day today, and…I wonder why. I just want to know if everything is OK." Elise, who was probably a gregarious, outgoing woman by nature, right now, struck Monica as completely uncertain, and stilted. Monica's heart thundered and a lump formed in her throat. But no way could she—or would she—open up. Not even a trace. Cracks in her weakening control system would explode beneath an onslaught of once tightly held emotion. Emotion Elise Edwards would never understand.

So, in essence, Monica ducked for cover. "Please don't worry," she said too brightly. "I'm just fine. I only wanted to…" She looked almost desperately toward the sanctuary of the deck. "Uh…"

Elise didn't bother stifling a sigh. Obviously disappointed, she shook her head. "Let me know if you need anything. Will we see you back at the table shortly?"

"Of course."

With that assurance, Elise left for the kitchen, but Monica wilted.

What a horrible way of reacting to the woman's hospitality, Monica thought, shamed and regretful at once. She had to escape—just for a minute, long enough to recapture her equilibrium. She moved quickly. Unlatching and opening the doors, she embraced the instant sense of peace and solitude. The spacious deck was empty now, cleared of furniture and accessories as winter dawned.

Don't be this way, she chided herself. *It's wrong. Self-pity won't change anything. Daveny and Kiara have every right to be thrilled. Furthermore, to do anything less than celebrate would hurt them and hurt Jeremy. He brought you here today for a reason. He wants you to become a deeper part of his life. It's an honor. Don't blow it!*

But the battle was like trying to beat back the whirling vortex of a tornado with nothing but smoke and mirrors.

She sank onto a set of steps that led to the backyard. She couldn't help admiring the gorgeous landscaping. Had to be the doing of both Elise and Daveny. Though winter rode in fast, groupings of hearty, large-headed mums still spotted the grounds with autumnal color. The grass remained thick and well-tended, a deep hue of green. Monica lost herself to the scent of burning wood that came from the chimney, the bracing chill of the wind. She quieted her mind. For about two or three seconds.

Why were others so abundantly blessed, as Ken put it, when by contradiction, her lot in this life was empty and barren in more ways than one? Why did others have it so easy—the relationships, the kids, the fulfilled lives, when that very destiny, the one she craved above all others, would never be hers to claim?

It was so easy to believe in God, and His blessings and grace, when your prayers were answered.

Dimly conscious of warm moisture on her cheeks, Monica blinked rapidly, aware now that tears fell from her eyes.

God, I hate feeling this way. It never ends, though. It never goes away. You don't seem to let it. Instead You always seem to narrow my world into a hyper-focus that leaves me seeing nothing else but what I lack, and everything I want so much but will never be able to have. Why?

Not much of a prayer, but right now, Monica didn't feel like God was much in the mood for listening—or answering her plea.

"Hey there, Jellybean. I thought this might come in handy right about now."

Jeremy.

Monica ducked her head and swiped fast at her cheeks. Meanwhile, from behind, he handed her a large, bistro mug of coffee. The warmth against her cold fingertips, and the fragrance, took a bit of the edge off her mood almost immediately.

Jeremy sat down next to her, silent, looking out upon the barren, wavering tree branches, the cloud-thickened sky. Monica stole a glance at him. A loose oxford shirt, comfortable jeans, lent him an air of casual appeal. Jeremy Blaise Edwards was impossibly handsome, but beyond that, he was finely attuned to the ones he loved, and he possessed a heart full of compassion and tenderness. Consequently, his presence in her life seemed yet another way God was letting her down.

Sure, she thought. *Show me the love, and promise, of a*

man like this. Tempt me with everything I want but can never possibly hold on to…then take it all away because I can never, ever be what he wants, and needs, the most.

"Thank you," she replied belatedly, but with genuine gratitude.

He looked into her eyes with that tantalizing quirk of a smile. The man left her aching, longing. Generally, she called the shots, and could perform breezy, graceful steps back when things got this complicated with a man. Not this time, though. *Why, why, why?*

"You're welcome, but I caught the vibe, Monica. I want to know what happened. Can you talk to me about whatever it is that's been bothering you today?"

She sighed out a puff of air. "JB, some things you can't change, or help with, no matter how much you may want to." She chewed on her lower lip and looked away.

"No," he murmured. "Not this time." Jeremy tucked a finger beneath her chin and tilted her head, directing her gaze to his. "Keep it right here." He stroked her cheek softly.

Such tenderness, so much caring. Every bit of the world she wanted was captured deep within his dark brown eyes. Those eyes were her undoing, and she backpedaled in fear. "I just needed some air. Really. No big deal, I promise."

"And that would be strike two, Monica." His irritation grew. She heard as much in his tone, and in the fact that Jellybean had reverted to Monica. "That makes twice you've backed away from me. Twice you've flat-out lied about something you're going through that's troubling. You did it at *Polonia*, and you're doing it now. Well, I'm right here, and I'm not going anywhere. Talk to me."

Her heart dissolved. Desire flowed hot, strong and tempting. But rationality entered the fray as well. "Not right now, OK? Not right this second. Not when your family is in the middle of a wonderful, happy celebration. I need to keep it together. Please understand."

"Fine. But, when I take you home tonight, we're going to talk." There was no room for negotiation. She breathed out heavily, and she stood, but Jeremy caught her hand and held it tight. From his perch on the deck stairs, he looked up at her while he caressed the back of her hand with his thumb. "Don't shut down. Not with me, and not with them." He indicated the people inside with a nod toward the house. "Share this with us. It's important. Because *you're* important."

Her chin quivered at his words. "Thanks. I appreciate it."

"Then like I said—don't close off." He stood smoothly, keeping her hand in his when they walked back inside.

10

While Jeremy focused on the drive to Monica's place, she shrank into the far side of the passenger seat and closed her eyes. Bracing herself, she prepared for the emotional blow she knew was coming. After all, following today's events, he had every right to be put out by her standoffish behavior. "Jeremy," she began timidly, "I'm so sorry I let you down."

No JB. No flirty sass. Instead, she stared straight ahead, into a curving roadway sided by towering trees. Homes, occasional stores, and strip malls flashed past. Silence pressed in on her from all sides, oppressive and nearly claustrophobic.

Sorry I let you down. Those five small words formed a haunting refrain, followed by the main verse: *And this is only the beginning.*

Jeremy turned into the entrance of Monica's subdivision. "I just don't get it. Kids are your passion. They're the largest part of your life. You love them. But today, with my family, and especially when Dav and Kiara made their announcements, when I figured you'd be one of the largest parts of the cheering section, you vanished. You sparkle, and you're so easy to be with, and enjoy. But today you backed yourself into a corner and not only did you refuse to leave that corner behind, you came off seeming—" He paused.

Shrugged. "Distant. You were defensive. For the life of me, I don't understand why."

His tone, laced by frustration, seeped into her system like some kind of slow-acting, destructive poison. The only anti-venom? Revelation.

They reached her home. When Jeremy parked, Monica looked straight ahead. "I didn't mean to be rude," she began, quietly. "I didn't want to feel the way I did today, Jeremy. I couldn't help it. I couldn't stop what came over me. I try, and I try…but…"

Jeremy touched her shoulder. His eyes glittered in the dim illumination of her neighbor's garage light. "Monica, what is it? Please tell me what's going on."

She squeezed her hands into tight fists. Before he could turn the tables, and gain an upper hand in this conversation, an upper hand she was in desperate need of maintaining, Monica exited his truck and walked into her home. Jeremy followed while she flicked on a couple lights and greeted Toby. After Toby leaped around Jeremy's legs, familiarizing himself with this intriguing stranger, and after the dog received a series of hearty pets and greetings, Monica released him into the backyard for a late-night romp so she could talk to Jeremy in peace.

As they sat on the couch in her living room, she began anew. "About today. First and foremost, let me repeat the fact that I'm sorry. Please know I didn't mean to hurt you, or anyone else."

"Apology accepted, Monica, but that's not even the issue for me right now. Not anymore. *You're* the issue. Something hurt you, and I want to know what it is. It's as simple as that."

"And as complicated," she whispered, blowing out a breath she held too tight in her chest. She spoke up louder now. "Actually I had a good time, but…"

Jeremy cut in. "But. *That's* the issue. Talk to me about *but.*"

Instinctively she looked up, searching his eyes. The degree of emotion she found there hit her senses, struck heat to her soul. The feelings between them had deepened with such heady speed. That fact alone wouldn't alarm her, but so much stood between them. All would be lost once he knew the truth about her, and that made everything about this day painful, and bittersweet.

"OK, let me try to get this out," she murmured, more to herself than Jeremy. She stood to pace the living room. In counterpoint, Jeremy remained seated. He seemed so calm. So rock steady.

"I enjoyed your family very much. They're funny and warm and loving. They're a symbol to me of everything you deserve, and probably long for in a family of your own. You told me yourself that you're mapping out a legacy. You want to keep tradition, and a family's love, alive in everything that you do. That's a beautiful thing."

"Monica, where is all of this coming from?" When she didn't answer right away, Jeremy persisted. "Let me in. Show me that you trust me."

She wrapped her arms around her waist, trying desperately to hold herself together while she took a sledgehammer to their relationship, a relationship she would have loved embracing. "You want children and a family more than anything, right?"

"Ultimately, yes. Absolutely."

"So do I." She spun toward him, desperate to avoid the fateful blow, but unable to stop it.

Jeremy waited, obviously not yet understanding

where the conversation was headed.

"But I can't be what you want. I'm not able. I can never get pregnant. I can never have children. I can't. I can't ever fill that part of your life—or my own. Your family is wonderful. That's honestly how I feel, even if I showed it poorly today. And family is of vital importance to you, Jeremy. That truth colored my entire time with them, and with you. It shredded a part of my heart, and my hopes for you and me."

His brows pulled together. He shook his head slightly and gave her a startled look. "What are you saying?"

"I'm infertile. The medical term for my condition is endometriosis. My case is severe enough that ultimately I may even require a hysterectomy."

His silence, hers coupled with it, allowed the charged air between them to settle a bit. Monica forced herself to take a few deep breaths to re-steady her trembling legs and hands.

She waited on him, stiff tension climbing up her back inch by fateful inch as the silence continued. She watched Jeremy blink free of his thoughts and lock focus on her face, then her eyes. "Wh…when? How did you find out? I mean—"

Monica stood stock still, facing him as straight as she could manage. "It's a long story."

"I've got time."

She remained frozen in place, in time. "It's got a lot of detail you may not want to hear."

"This is your life, right? The battle you're fighting?"

She nodded.

"Then don't cushion me. Or us. There's nothing about you that I *don't* want to hear about, or know about. Believe that."

The *us* portion of that sentence sounded so good. In fact, it skimmed against her skin like the stroke of a sable brush.

"OK. For better or worse." She paused. "When I"—she shrugged delicately—"came of age physically, I had issues from day one. Symptoms started small, but built, year-by-year, until by the time I was halfway through college, I had it all. The swollen stomach. Nausea. Blinding headaches. Excessive bleeding. To cap it all off, the middle of every blessed month was an odyssey of pain." Memories crashed in—leaving her feeling so bereft. So unfeminine, and immodest. That's why she could discuss the condition with Jeremy now. She had been forced to become clinical about it all. Detached. Except when in the company of large, loving families. Expanding families. Being with the Edwards's today filled her with an ache so acute, so pervasive, it knocked the very breath right out of her.

But she had to tell him everything. She could accept no other option but complete honesty. "My condition became severe enough that I finally sought help. I went to specialists. For months, I lived an honest-to-goodness nightmare when it came to my health. I won't go into the ways in which I felt like a guinea pig, or like I was nothing more than a test specimen. At the end of almost a year, after blood tests, hormone treatments, a laparoscopy, and at last, full-blown surgery, the best they could come up with was that I suffered from ovarian cysts which I had a possibility of outgrowing at some point in the future."

Monica paced, unable to meet his gaze right now. "The process was humiliating, but I was young and figured I had hope. In the meantime, I found my calling with early childhood education. Maybe something inside my head was getting the message my heart refused to accept—that I better prepare myself for life without kids of my own by building my life around those I *could* help, and teach and engage."

Jeremy stood, and he did the pacing now. "Are you sure kids are out of the question? From what very little I know about endometriosis, it's inconsistent, isn't it? Women can still get pregnant, still have happy, healthy babies—right?"

The longing in his voice was a near perfect echo of her own. She understood completely because she lived those desires day by day, month after month, until hope became exhausted. She didn't even try to cushion her answer. "Not this time. Not for me."

Those six quietly spoken words hung in the air.

"You can't hold any illusions about me, Jeremy. I'm beaten, and I'm scared, and I'm angry. I don't even feel…" She shrugged and looked up at the ceiling to blink her blurred vision clear of moisture. "I don't even feel feminine sometimes." She faced him squarely. "I've been told in counseling that that may be part of why I focus on dance and physical expression—to affirm my time and place as a woman. I just don't know anymore. And I most certainly don't want to wake up to feelings like I have for you, then go through a crash and burn when the relationship dissolves because I can't be everything you want, and need. The idea of that scares me to death. I've been denied so much—so many things that my heart holds most dear. I know how selfish and narcissistic that sounds, but my feelings are my feelings, and I can't escape them, no matter how hard I try." She hung her head, returning to the couch.

Jeremy joined her.

"I'm so sorry for backing off from everything, and everyone, today. But can you possibly understand how Daveny and Kiara's announcement cut through my heart? How being around your family affected me?"

He studied her for a moment before answering. "Yes, Monica, I can. But the only way you're going to get to the other side of this situation is by grabbing hold of some semblance of faith, and trust. Learn to let go of what God is denying you, and focus instead on everything He's given you!"

She'd been down this road before, and she was ready. "Really?" She fired back. "What has He given me? I'm empty! I'm literally and figuratively empty! How can that appeal to you—in the long term? Once the passion and excitement is replaced by the day-to-day, how will you be able to be happy with a woman who can't give you a family? A woman who can't give you a child, and the legacy you've admitted to building your life for?"

"Thanks for shortchanging me, Monica. Thanks a lot."

"Jeremy, listen to what I'm *saying*! Be *realistic*! This is as much about how inadequate I feel as it is about my feelings for you!"

"OK, then let me be realistic." He stood and turned to her. He met her hot and confrontational posture straight on. "In fact, here's a healthy dose of realism for you: do you think you're not benefiting every single child at Sunny Horizons? What about the girls who dance for you? What about them? Don't any of them count in the balance?"

Monica gaped. "Well there we go. Problem solved!"

"Monica, stop it!"

"No, *you* stop it! First of all, the answer to my problems is *not* that simple. Secondly, even the point of view you just expressed doesn't answer what I'm unable to bring to a relationship, to a family life, with you or anyone else over the long term."

"So your answer is to give up? Really? That's so not like the woman I've gotten to know, and admire."

"It's not giving up, it's being realistic." Monica tried to steady her breathing; she leaned forward and cradled her head in her hands. "I've been operated on by scalpels and lasers, spent portions of the month flat on my back, endured tests and needles, been treated with drugs and still endured the pain. At the end of the road the truth is this: I'm not meant to have a family. I've had to find a way to accept that."

"Monica, you're one of the strongest women I've ever met. You're good hearted and intelligent—smart enough to recognize stubbornness! You're suffering from tunnel vision."

"Tunnel vision." She shook her head. "I guess that's how you'd see it. I suppose it's easy to downplay what I feel, and the emptiness that goes along with it." Then, since they were at the point of no return anyhow, she admitted to the worst of her doubts and fears. "I feel like I was marked as unworthy. Less of a woman."

He studied her in silence for a long, tense moment. "You couldn't be more wrong."

She shook her head, making an exasperated noise. She looked up in time to see Jeremy squeeze the bridge of his nose.

"You know, I could talk until I'm blue in the face, but you won't realize the truth of what I'm saying until you find a way to take a long, hard look at the life you really have in front of you versus the life you're clinging to despite everything God's showing you!"

"Once again, Jeremy, you're using platitudes to simplify what I feel—and I'm here to tell you, it just doesn't work! It sounds great in theory, sure, but that philosophy has failed me miserably." Almost immediately, she regretted those snapping words, and her waspish tone.

Her attitude didn't seem to deter him in the least, though. Jeremy possessed the ability to recognize pain versus anger. Further, he cared—cared enough to endure the sword slice of her self-doubts. So when he took a deep breath, and returned to her side at the couch, Monica welcomed his touch—the way he held her shoulders fast, but with tenderness.

And he urged, "*Please* don't make this your life's deal breaker. You're better than that. You're an exquisite, remarkable woman. And you have too many gifts to offer this world, and the children in it, to let this beat you, or close you down. Anything less is a waste."

The words slipped past her defensive walls and struck home, giving her a lot to think about. Jeremy continued. "One last thing to consider, Monica – and I want you to understand this fact with complete clarity: passion and fire may cool, but they never disappear. My *feelings* for you won't disappear. If you're waiting for that to happen—expecting it to happen because of infertility—then you'll end up disappointed. I told you at *Polonia*, I'm a man of action. I'm about resolving things—good and bad—by being present to the people I care about. I don't disappear. I don't vanish in the face of what I do, or don't, receive in this life. My blessings come from God—and you're just that to me,

Monica Kittelski. You're precious. To me. To God. Accept that fact. Deal with it."

His tough-minded declaration stirred her senses. Her blood sang, pounding in her ears. Tears poured down her cheeks, a sudden and unstoppable flood of release and longing. "I'm scared, and I *hate* being scared. I blew it today, and I know it. I didn't mean to. Honest. Thing is, I don't know how to move ahead without screwing up, JB. And I do *not* want to screw this up." The resumption of his nickname came easy just now.

He relaxed his shoulders a bit and took her hands in his. "I told you before, I'm not good with the words, with putting emotions forward," he said quietly. "But I know who is. Would you please, for me, talk this over with Ken? I promise you he'll provide objective advice. He's been through heartbreaks that are different from yours, but just as powerful, and he's a remarkable man. I trust him completely, and he will *not* pressure you. You don't have to claim God. Not yet, if you're not ready and able—but give a try to *listening* to God. I believe in His providence with all my heart, Monica. Pour your heart out, and I promise, in His hands, you'll be safe. You'll be cared for. Would you do that? For me?"

"For us?" she asked with a shaky voice and a trembling that was probably easy for him to see, given her tight stance.

"For us."

"I can only try."

His eyes dimmed. "Trying is fine, Monica, but you can't bolt in the face of what you've been denied, like you did today. That worries me a lot more than whether or not you can have kids. Get a handle on that part of your battle, OK? More than a mother to my children, I want a woman who will stand by my side — no matter *what* — knowing our strength, and provision, will come from Christ, and that in that faith will come goodness. Lean on Him, Jellybean, or your troubles will only intensify. You've been bearing the load on your own for way too long. You need, and deserve, His grace. It's perfect, and it's faultless, no matter what your outward circumstances appear. The time-worn cliché is so very true: when we can't, God can. Will you talk to Ken?"

She deflected her gaze, but slowly — very slowly — she nodded.

11

"I'm not saying I don't like Monica, JB. That's not my point at all!"

"That's not the way it seems to me right now, Mom."

Just days after Sunday dinner with his parents, Jeremy found himself the subject of a motherly debriefing. She knew he usually spent Tuesdays and Thursdays at the offices of Edwards Construction in a grudging concession to company bureaucracy, so she paid him a visit, the subject matter of said visit, his girlfriend.

His mother sat across from his desk in the utilitarian office he occupied. Just down the hall was a second office for the bookkeeper, Paula Cromwell, and out front sat the receptionist and Jane-of-all-trades, Allison Moynah. The duo comprised his corporate team, and they were housed in a small business office along Jefferson Avenue.

He stretched back in his chair, doing his best to absorb the crux of her comments without becoming angry, or defensive. "So can you clarify what *are* you saying, Mom? Because what should be a pleasant get-together is starting to feel more like an inquisition."

When his mom had called Monday and asked to meet, Jeremy had embraced the opportunity. Now he wasn't as enthusiastic. Tension crept through the muscles of his shoulders. His fingertips twitched with a pen; he clicked and tapped it while he sat, and waited.

His mother temporarily embraced the silence, then continued. "JB, she's nice enough, I suppose, and certainly she's as attractive as can be, but I don't know, she seems remote. Shuttered. She's very guarded. It's like she was uncomfortable for some reason. I guess I'm surprised she holds such strong appeal to a family man like you when all she wanted to do all day was hide."

That comment struck a chord. All he could think of, all he could see in his mind's eye was Monica's defeat, her sadness and the futility she experienced. She was lost right now, and he cared for her. Therefore, abandonment was not an option. He wanted to stand up for her. "Mom, trust me when I say there are circumstances that can cause even the most wonderful person to stumble, and hold back."

Her eyes sharpened. "And this family knows that better than most, JB—especially after what Collin, and all of us, endured after Lance was killed."

Jeremy sighed, sipping from the mug of coffee before him. Elise's ginger tea steamed nearby, thus far untouched. More and more he realized this visit wasn't about catching up, it was about probing. "True, Mom, and I appreciate your protectiveness. But show some compassion as well. Show her some leeway and understanding. She has a few things she's working out." He couldn't bring himself to be as open and blunt with his mother as Monica had been with him. Not yet. Not when quicksand shifted and pulled all around.

"All right, all right—but still, I just don't know

what to make of her."

"Meaning?"

She leaned back, crossing her legs and finally sipping from her mug. "For example, she loves kids, but this past weekend, she wanted nothing to do with them. She owns a daycare center, for heaven's sake, but we had to force her to play a few simple board games with the kids, and join in the soccer game."

Jeremy went stiff. His mom made valid points. Her honest, though blunt observations were on the mark, but they only served to stir his disquiet, and increase his understanding of the undercurrents that had affected Monica's mood that day. So, once more, he stepped forward to be a buffer. "Daveny and Collin are excellent judges of character, and so am I. Trust in that, OK?" After a calming pause, Jeremy felt better. Shifting aside a half-unrolled set of blueprints, he retrieved a stack of job files and made ready to dive back into paperwork. And he bluffed just a bit. "As to avoidance, maybe she was looking forward to a little adult company and conversation. Remember, she's with kids almost twenty-four seven. She may have wanted, and needed, a bit of a breather from the pitter-patter, know what I mean?"

"Yes, to a degree, but I think there's more to it. You've said you're talking about it. Working it through. If that's the case, then I'm happy. I promise I'll leave my overly protective fingers out of the mix. I don't mean to be so rough on her, or you, but I worry about my kids. It's wired into my DNA. Always has been, always will be. If she has your heart, then she'll have mine as well. No question."

She hadn't been thrown off the scent, but her final words were just what he expected, and hoped, from his mother. A twisted knot of anxiety and tension loosened its grip from the base of his neck. Jeremy reached across the desk and squeezed her hand. "Thanks."

"You're very much like your father. You're quiet about your emotions, but you carry them deep, and your feelings are strong. I'm only speaking up because I don't want to see you get hurt."

Jeremy took a quick mental walk through the past few days. Monica had stepped forward, albeit tentatively. After all, she had spoken freely, and frankly, about her condition. She had taken custody of Ken's phone number on a promise to connect with Woodland's pastor. From there, Jeremy toyed with the idea of including her in this weekend's services as well and decided it would be a good idea to extend an invitation.

Inviting her to Woodland on Sunday would establish a point of comfort for Monica with the church and its atmosphere before she met with Ken. It would also show his family, once again, his intent and seriousness. He wanted Monica to find God's mercy. He wanted her to feel acceptance. Within the embrace of Woodland Church, she might make a way to God, to being affirmed.

His mother leaned forward setting aside her tea in a smooth, deliberate way. Her sea-green eyes narrowed just a bit, but she smiled. "She means a great deal to you."

"Yes." No need to embellish. For a millisecond he considered the emptiness Monica felt. The insecurity. It tore him apart inside. Jeremy refused to add to her sense of pain and insecurity. This relationship merited solid footing and every fighting chance.

Indeed, she meant that much.

"I see it all in your eyes," his mother said quietly. She left it at that, giving his arm a gentle pat.

Jeremy played it close to the vest, and kept it to himself that he intended to take her to church on Sunday. He also kept quiet about his intention to invite her to Rebecca's wedding. Despite well-meaning, motherly intrusion, Elise Edwards knew her children well. She was right when she said he didn't play cavalier with his emotions. He wanted to establish firm footing with Monica. Nothing else mattered.

❧

Jeremy had to admit, he felt out of place.

It was Wednesday night. About a half-dozen women were gathered outside the doorway of the Saint Clair Shores Community Center. They looked inside, bragging proudly about their daughters, who currently practiced ballet. He belonged here like a square peg in a round hole.

Hanging back, he watched the class taking place inside, smiling while he watched Monica spin, stretch, and form her arms into a perfect arc above her head.

"Monica is so good with the girls. I wonder if she has any kids of her own."

The comment came from one of the moms who peered inside, and it won Jeremy's attention.

"I'm not sure," a second parent answered. "I wonder if she's married. She doesn't wear a wedding ring." A pause followed that remark. "One thing is for sure," she added, "if Monica weren't so nice, I'd hate her."

A third woman chuckled. "I know what you

mean. No woman should have blonde hair, blue eyes, and that much grace. It's disgusting. Just watch her."

That's exactly what Jeremy did. Throughout the last few minutes of class, Monica coached the little girls along, performing the ballet routine along with them. Each lift of her arms, each dip and sway, was executed with a smoothness that could never be taught. Fluid grace like hers was innate, and it textured each of her movements, even beyond the dance floor.

The song came to an end, and she concluded class for the week. Monica looked toward the doorway. After she delivered a smile and a wave, the waiting parents entered the room. Still chatting amiably, adults laid claim to their young dancers who charged forward eagerly after bidding Monica good night.

When the noise and activity died down, Jeremy slipped inside. Monica's back was to him as she stashed one set of CDs and retrieved another. She picked up a water bottle and drank deep, which left Jeremy with a definite sensual vibration. When she patted a towel against her neck and shoulders, he stepped up. He hid his hands, and a treat, behind his back.

"Hey, Miss Monica." His playful call caused her to freeze for a moment, then she turned, her eyes alight with happiness and affection. Jeremy smiled and gave her a slow wink. A bit closer now, he moved his hands from their hiding position, revealing that he held a single, long-stemmed pink rose. Attached to the stem, via a white, curled ribbon was a small bag of jellybeans. "For the teacher."

Monica accepted with a blush that almost perfectly matched the hue of the flower. "Thanks, JB."

Just like that, he found himself the willing target of

her large, luminous eyes. A wisp of golden hair slid over the hollow in her shoulder. Jeremy watched its trail, mesmerized. Following an hour of dance instruction, her skin glowed, radiant with health.

"You were quite the topic of conversation out in the hallway." He itched to reach up and twirl that silky curl of hair around his finger. "The moms out there are about ready to start a fan club."

Monica laughed. "Stop it!"

"I'm serious. Rumor has it they're headed out to get t-shirts printed up." Her second round of laughter played like music, tickling his senses. "They love you."

"They're just a really nice group. They seem to appreciate what I do with the girls."

"The moms aren't the only ones who are captivated." That caused Monica to look away shyly, which left Jeremy all the more eager to heighten her awareness. "I watched you just now. You're as graceful in body as you are in spirit."

As hoped, the flush ripened, and she turned away, kneeling. She placed the rose and candy gently next to her tote. Still, Monica was Monica, and when she stood, she quickly recovered her playful *élan*. "And how sweet are you—coming all the way out here just to tell me that, and deliver a treat? What's the occasion?"

"I have a proposal to make." He'd created the opening he wanted. "How do you stand on the topic of church?"

Monica gave him an inquiring look. "I like church just fine. Why?"

A pony-tailed young lady with big brown eyes and peaches-and-cream skin interrupted them. The little girl dashed up and hugged Monica's legs. "Bye,

Miss Monica. See you tomorrow at school. Thank you for helping me practice today."

He watched Monica quite literally dissolve under the youngster's loving regard. She ran her fingertips against the straight, silky strands of the girl's chestnut colored hair and she hugged the child right back. "It's my absolute pleasure, Jessica. I'm so proud of the progress you've made! See you tomorrow."

Wearing a great smile, Jessica ran off. Following a brief look into Monica's eyes, Jeremy tracked the girl's progress to the outside hallway where her mother waited. The mom gave Monica a wave along with a tired, but happy smile. "That wouldn't happen to be the pair you were talking about at dinner the other night?

Monica kept an eye on the pair and nodded. "Yeah, sorry for being so scant on the details when we talked, but I always try to be careful when it comes to confidentiality issues."

Jeremy took her hand and swung it loosely. "Relationships mean intimacy. Intimacy means revelation—and the situation was bothering you. I won't compromise that show of trust, Monica. It's part of growing together."

She stretched up on tip-toe and kissed Jeremy's cheek; her eyes came alive with tender affection. "I appreciate that, because it's hard to keep lines from blurring when you…ah…"

Jeremy chuckled at her stutter. "Develop into a couple?"

She blushed and moistened her lips. But then, she nodded. "To answer your question a bit more directly, that's Jessica and Caroline Dempsey, and I think they're going to be OK. I really do."

"Good. She looks like a precious little girl."

"She is, but I'm sorry for the interruption."

"Not a problem at all."

Monica's focus centered in, and she tilted her head. "You were asking me about church."

"Yes. I was wondering—do you think you could join me for services at Woodland this Sunday?"

Her eyes went a bit wide. She tilted her head and leaned back a bit "I, ah...JB, really...I appreciate you including me. That's so thoughtful, I enjoy church and everything. I'm a little worried, though, and...and it's your family, and I'm just not sure...Would it be right? Would I fit in, and..."

He pressed a fingertip against her lips to still her speed talking, warmed by the fact that he now recognized the nervous habit. He waited a moment for her to be still. "One step at a time, Jellybean," he murmured. "One brick at a time."

Her shoulders sagged. Her eyes went soft, and plaintive. "But I'm embarrassed."

"About what?"

"About facing your family again. They probably don't even like me much, and I can't honestly say I blame them."

"Don't fear that road; walk down it instead. My family is about care, and love. They get protective, and intrusive, yes, but they're also very quick to forgive, and ask forgiveness in return. They care. They don't understand all your battles yet, but they know what happened this weekend isn't about them, or how you feel about them. I promise you that."

"How do you know, JB? How can you be so sure?"

"Because I already talked it over with my mom."

Monica's mouth opened and closed.

He chuckled. "We don't let things fester or go unquestioned, and unresolved. The Edwards clan moves forward. And, my mom is as tough as they come, but she knows, without question now, how important you are to me. That's what's called a deal breaker."

Jeremy looked down and took hold of her hand, oddly touched by the sight of their fingertips entwined. His flesh, slightly darker, seemed such a striking contrast to her fair, creamy skin. "We're scrappy and affectionate and we take no prisoners. Kinda like a certain exquisite lady I'm quite fond of who teaches little girls about grace and beautiful movement, and teaches kids about the rules of school, and life. Know what I mean?"

He could see her reaction in the shallow fall of her breathing, the wide, questing expression on her face as the words he spoke hit home. The pink leotard she wore was snug, but discreet, with a slight, scooped neckline. Her ensemble included a short matching skirt of rippling silk that floated around her legs with each move she made, each breath of air.

"You were wrong, JB, when you said you aren't any good with words. You keep showing me how gifted you are in that regard." She nibbled her lower lip. He longed to reach out and stroke the corner of her mouth until she relaxed.

"Thanks, Jellybean."

"I made the call yesterday. To Pastor Ken. I'm seeing him next week, on Tuesday, after work. I want you to know that. I did it because you're important to me, too."

Hope performed a vigorous dance through his blood stream. She was hesitant—he recognized that clearly—but she looked up at him in eagerness for approval. Jeremy was so happy she had made that difficult first step, and he wanted to help make that forward motion as easy on her as possible. "Then it seems to me like timing is everything. If you can come with me on Sunday, you'll get to see what Woodland's all about. Maybe spending some time at church, seeing Ken and the family again, will help you feel a lot better about things, and more comfortable when you meet with him."

"I'm sure it will." She fidgeted with the ends of the satin tie of her skirt, which was fashioned into a bow at her waist. "I'd like to go with you."

The moment was broken by the arrival of her second class of dance students, this group slightly older than the last. The girls filtered into the room, full of noisy greetings and laughter. Jeremy stepped away, but kept hold of her hand for as long as he could. He released her at last. "Bye, Jellybean."

She watched after him for a moment. "Call me later?"

Jeremy thought about that for a second or two. "I'll do you one better. Can I tempt you with dessert after class?"

"Cold Stone ice cream?" she requested expectantly.

Jeremy just grinned, and arched a brow. "I'll take that as a yes. Class is done at eight?"

"Yep. I'll meet you there."

Jeremy left the room and closed the door quietly as Monica began class.

"I'm impressed." Jeremy stared at Monica with wide eyes.

Monica sat back comfortably in the curved back, metal chair of the small table they shared inside the ice cream shop. She smiled victoriously because her paper cup, formerly overflowing with an order of chocolate peanut butter, was now empty. "Two scoops goes down *so* well after a ballet session."

"Let me follow you home. Make sure you get in OK."

"What?"

"You heard me."

"JB, I'm a capable, intelligent woman who's gone home alone thousands of times. I'll be fine."

"But it's dark, and it's cold. Call me old-fashioned. I want to see you home." More to the point, he wanted a pitch-black night to surround them, full of the promise of snow; and he wanted kisses—dewy, warm, soul-saturating, provocative goodnight kisses.

Monica picked up the cup and spooned out the very last remnants of her gourmet ice cream treat. She licked the utensil clean, her gaze narrow when she looked up at him once more. "Are you sure you're not a closet chauvinist?"

"Positive. Now, indulge me."

"It's out of your way."

"By two whole miles. How will I *ever* find a way to justify the fossil fuel emissions?"

Monica burst out laughing. "Oh man—and this game is over. You win."

"Besides, think of the convenience. I'll be able to help you carry in all that equipment from class. Now. Are you done, or are you going to go after that last little dribble of chocolate right there on the side of the cup—"

"Shut up," she admonished through giggles, diverting her gaze as she went after that last little dribble of chocolate right there on the side of the cup.

They left the shop hand in hand, strolling slowly to their parked cars. After following Monica home, he walked her to the door, carrying the stereo and duffle bag.

"I've decided. You're not a closet chauvinist. Rather, you're openly chivalrous," Monica set aside her ballet class supplies.

The beckoning warmth of her eyes, the curve of her lips, were his undoing.

Jeremy moved slowly, but with purpose. He took hold of her hands as he pressed forward, pinning them next to her head when he landed her back against the wall of the porch. The rough feel of brick against his hands, the chill, the scent of burning wood and snow to come, combined into a heady sensation and atmosphere.

He dipped his head and her warmth, her scent, swirled through him. Jeremy's resistance snapped. He claimed her mouth with delicious desire, devouring her every answering response. Against his chest, he could have sworn he felt the thundering of her heart— or perhaps it was his own. The connection worked magic, ignited fire, provoked his senses. He bent to its power, then fell headlong before he even knew what hit.

This was possession, soul-deep and irrevocable. The realization glided through him. He gave a throaty sound, releasing her hands so his fingertips could take a dive through her now loosened hair. Monica sank heavily against the wall, and he flattened his hands against cold, gritty brick. The effort somehow tethered him to reality. Just barely.

She sighed as she took hold of his arms and continued to kiss him senseless. His body formed a cover against hers, like a perfect, well-honed shield. With a last sound of wrangled desire, JB stepped back. His breathing was shallow. "Take out your keys." He almost growled the words, needing to put some distance between them before his senses overtook his rationale.

"Huh?" Her eyes were glazed and heavy.

He traced her jaw with a fingertip. "Take out your keys. I want to make sure you get in before I leave." He looked her straight in the eye, knowing his battles were visible. Still, he maintained restraint. "I need to leave."

Only then did he realize Monica's purse now resided on the ground at her feet. It had slid off her shoulder, unnoticed. Before she could move, JB bent smoothly and retrieved it for her, handing it over—though he kept a safe measure of physical distance between them.

"Ah—thanks." Her voice, of smoothest whiskey, stirred a warm throb of life, a shivering echo of their touch, their kiss.

"Inside," he directed once more, his own voice husky, and abrupt. The only thing that kept him from stepping over a moral boundary was his inbred belief system, and the pure sense of reverence he felt toward her.

"Inside," she murmured in agreement, fumbling for her keys. It took two tries, but the key found home in her doorknob. Inside, Toby went nuts. She swung the door wide, clicking on a nearby light switch. The dog bounded forward, jumping, grunting, wagging his tail. Light, sound and Monica's exuberant pet helped dissipate a few more of Jeremy's mental fog curls. He made quick work of greeting his new four-legged friend, and set the remainder of Monica's gear inside the entryway.

When he walked down the porch steps, Monica looked back at him and said softly, "See ya.'"

He turned, intending to give a wave. *Tempting. So tempting.* Instead, Jeremy buried his hands deep in the pockets of his leather jacket to keep himself in check.

"You knock me out, Jellybean," he murmured. "You absolutely knock me out. See ya.'"

12

Sunday morning, Jeremy walked through the doors of Woodland Church hand in hand with Monica. He edged them toward the etched glass doors to the sanctuary, which were presently flung open to welcome one and all to ten o'clock services. Jeremy was stopped repeatedly by people he knew, but he didn't mind. It gave him the chance to mix and mingle with Monica at his side, and introduce her to his place of worship.

They moved through the entrance and down the main aisle to join his family. Jeremy was about to slide into the pew, next to his mother, but Monica restrained him by taking hold of his arm. She moved smoothly ahead, claiming that spot instead. Following a deliberate glance into Jeremy's eyes, Monica sat.

"Good morning, Elise," she said. "How are you?" She leaned forward to make eye contact with his father as well. "Hi, Ben. It's good to see you again."

Genuine and welcoming, Monica possessed top-notch intuition. Jeremy warmed on the inside, proud of her. Monica seemed eager that any residual discomfort from last weekend vanished, and her efforts didn't go unnoticed. His mother didn't bubble over, like usual, or offer one of her automatic hugs, but she smiled and handed Monica a hymnal and a brief discussion ensued regarding the rundown of the day's readings and order of service.

It was a positive start, and Jeremy telegraphed that recognition into physicality, placing his arm along the back of the pew, keeping a connected, protective touch on Monica's shoulder.

Afterwards, they hung back to spend some time talking with family members and friends. Ken was deluged with departing parishioners, so one-on-one time with the pastor seemed out of the question for the time being—especially when one church member, an elderly lady who was speaking with Ken intently, ended up being led to his office after services. Looked like Ken's help was required elsewhere today.

Jeremy didn't mind much, however. Monica had made an entrée into his life at Woodland with genuine comfort. Hope bloomed.

After church, it was time to bond with his brothers. He dropped Monica at her place, made a mad dash home to change clothes. He'd soon be on his way to Ford Field for a Detroit Lion's football game.

Monica's introduction to Woodland was a success, however a new realization dawned. What got lost in translation of late was his own reaction to falling so hard, and so fast, for a woman who would never be able to carry a child. His child. *Their* child.

Was it crazy to think so far ahead? The practical side of his nature said yes, but his heart screamed no—loud and clear.

Definitely a topic for discussion with his most trusted confidantes—his brothers.

A short time later, he and his brothers were on the road, headed into downtown Detroit. And it didn't take long for those trusted confidantes to gang up on him. In fact, the tag team event began almost immediately.

"So, bro," Marty began, "you hearing the call of the ball and chain? You getting ready to take that fateful plunge?"

From the rear seat, Jeremy looked at his watch. "Wow, Marty. That only took three minutes. Coll, you had even money on five minutes. I had greater faith in his lack of restraint and pegged that question coming in at seven minutes after pick-up."

Riding shotgun, Collin turned to look over his shoulder. His grin went devilish. "Sorry, JB, but I'm with Marty on this one. Next thing you know, you'll be strolling the aisles of some high-end department store with one of those radar guns, electro-registering for flatware and china patterns. It's a sad day, really. The end of a legend."

Jeremy openly gaped at Collin, the one he had expected to be his champion. "Way to perform a stand up, Coll. Let's hope the Lions defensive line shows more skill than you."

"Touchy, touchy," Marty quipped. "Might as well give in, JB. Monica's great. Steph said she's real nice. She enjoyed spending time with her."

That was good to hear. "Thanks. Mom's a bit of a tougher nut to crack on that count, though. I think she came away a little disappointed. And concerned. Her expectations were different than what Monica showed last weekend. Especially with the kids."

By intent, the sentence dangled, creating a means by which to seek their counsel on the issue of children, and family. Marty was shrewd, and perceptive, too. He picked up on the undercurrent with ease. "I kinda noticed that. In the backyard, during that soccer scrimmage."

Collin nodded. "St. Antoine Street garage is coming up."

Their conversation on hold now, Marty pulled up to the gate of the parking structure and swiped a ticket from the dispenser. From there, walking into Ford Field was akin to facing a blitzkrieg of sound, sensation and excitement. The crowd hummed, speakers blared music with a pounding beat that synched with digital ads and crowd-sparking prompts that formed a never-ending circle of lights and color across the mid-section of the stadium.

After stocking up on food and drinks, they took their seats and settled in. They sent up a unison roar of support at kick-off when the Lions took possession and performed a decent, 30-yard return. After a while, the game evolved into a back-and-forth rhythm that enabled Jeremy to join his brothers in simply stretching back, downing some junk food, and chatting.

The Lions and Packers were locked in a three-three tie at the end of the first quarter. Jeremy put out a test comment as he surveyed the cheering crowd that surrounded them. "This is the best. And I love watching the families."

"We gotta train 'em young to appreciate the joys and agonies of pro football in Detroit," Collin answered, tossing back a handful of popcorn and propping his feet against the chair in front of him.

"Pro?" Marty shot back. "You sure about that?"

Jeremy's eyes narrowed. "The Lions are hanging tough. Have faith." He bit into his hotdog and chewed, pondering for a bit. "Have you ever thought about what your life would be like without kids?"

If surprised by the question, Marty and Collin didn't show it.

"Nope. Once you have them, you can't remember a time when they weren't a part of your life," Marty said.

"They change everything, for sure," Collin added.

Jeremy's intensity increased by small degrees. "Yeah, but"—he stopped watching the game and instead, regarded his brothers—"what if you weren't able to have them? What if Stephanie couldn't have conceived? What if Daveny were infertile? Would it have made a difference to you? You know, in your relationship?"

Marty and Collin exchanged a look, then gave Jeremy their complete attention. Collin leaned in. "It would have been a tough thing to consider, I have to say that, but I also have to say nothing would change the love I feel for Daveny. It's that powerful a thing."

"Same here. I can't imagine my life without Steph. But it would have taken some serious help to overcome. Some serious prayer time and heart-to-heart."

"Tell me about it," Jeremy muttered, trying to keep track of the action on the field. Players, uniforms, downs all became a blur.

"What are you saying, JB?" Collin asked. "What's up? Does this have to do with Monica, somehow?"

Jeremy speared his brother with a look. Come clean? Protect their privacy as a couple? He wasn't quite sure what to do, but these were his brothers, his allies. "Monica can't have kids. She can't conceive."

Despite the noise level of the game, a stillness settled between the threesome. Glances were exchanged as Jeremy's revelation was absorbed.

"So, that's what these questions are all about." Marty's eyebrows lifted, and he blew out a sigh. "Gotta say, that's a tough one, JB. What's the issue? Why can't she have kids?"

"Ever hear of endometriosis?"

Compassion glimmered through Marty's eyes. Collin frowned.

"She's had it for years. It's serious enough that she'll never be able to have kids of her own." He filled them in with a bit of background.

When he was through, Marty seemed to check in with Collin. "Listen up, JB," Marty began. "You want some input from my end? Stick by her. She's good for you. I've never seen you look at a woman with love in your eyes. You've never let your heart go. Not completely. Now you have. You've got Monica, and you're happy. I could tell that as soon as I saw the two of you together on Sunday."

A bomb blast could have taken place at mid-field and Jeremy wouldn't have noticed. His focus latched onto Marty and stayed put.

"All I'll add is that you can't let her condition stand in the way," Collin put in. "Not if she's the one. If you do, you'll lose the woman you're meant to be with."

The Lions must have done something great on the field, because the crowd sent up a yell that resounded through the stadium. When the cheering abated, Jeremy admitted, "I don't know if I can take it, guys. I want a family. I want kids. I want a houseful of noise and love like we grew up in. With Monica I'd have to give up that dream."

Collin paused, then looked Jeremy straight in the eyes. "And Monica?"

Jeremy stared at him blankly.

Collin sighed, and shook his head. "What about

Monica? What about *her* dreams? You've told us just now how important kids are to her, and I see her day after day at Sunny Horizons. I can tell how much she loves them. This isn't just your dream, JB. It's hers, too."

"Yeah, you're right." Jeremy's reply came out tinged by heat because Collin's observation placed him smack-dab between love and heart-felt wishes. "Her needs, my needs, they're tough to reconcile, all things considered, know what I mean? That's my problem!"

"You bet I know what you mean," Marty said. "And we're on your side—but maybe what the two of you need to do is see all the alternatives available—all the opportunities you have to pursue a family outside of traditional, natural means."

"Adoption," Jeremy said.

"Adoption," Collin and Marty answered.

Jeremy pursed his lips and looked, unseeing, at the carpet of green field before him. He focused enough to recognize the Lions now led by a field goal. So that had been the cause of ruckus just a bit ago. "I hate to even raise the issue. She's emotionally and physically exhausted. To be honest, I think she's done trying to deal with family issues. Instead, she's pouring her energy into the daycare center and her dance classes at the community center."

Collin leaned forward on his knees. His attention centered on the field, but his eyes were cloudy, distant. "I can understand that method of coping. She's trying to convince herself she's fulfilled. That everything is OK in her life. I used to practice that kind of evasion about Lance, until Daveny, and God's plan, entered my life and turned it completely around. Maybe that's the role you're meant to play in Monica's life, bro. A catalyst. A lifeline, as well as a partner."

Marty took it from there. "I'll bottom line it for ya,' JB. Do you love Monica enough to forego the single life, *and* family? She's unable to have kids. If she's dead set against adoption once you guys talk it over, you'll need to make that decision."

Marty's observation was on the mark. Jeremy swigged back some soda and crunched some popcorn. "I can't help how I feel. I want a family. I've worked hard to build Edwards Construction into a source of provision, a company I can maybe pass on to my kids someday, or at least see to their security as they grow up. That's part of what drives me. Part of what I am."

Collin gave him a sharp look. "Fair enough. But don't sacrifice your heart for that. If you do, you'll end up miserable. Provision, and legacies, are great, but they won't fill that empty spot you're talking about."

"But—"

"But *nothing*," Marty chimed in. "You may not be able to have it both ways—Monica and a family, too. Figure out what you want, sort it out and build from there. Time will win her trust. Your support—and it can't waver—will do the rest."

A course to follow. Back to basics.

Marty started to pay attention to the action on the field. He sent up a happy whoop that drew them all back into the game. "First down, baby!"

Collin and JB exchanged smirks.

"Don't fall into the trap, Marty. Remember, it's the Lions." Collin slapped Marty on the shoulder.

Marty looked at Collin with a determined glint in his eye. "And remember, like JB said, hope springs eternal."

৵৽

At home that night, Jeremy's restless mind refused to calm. He changed into sweats, tried to unwind. Instead, he paced.

In the end, he stood before golden, slowly-dying embers in his fireplace, studying a lineup of photographs along the mantle. He reached out, picking up one of the framed pictures. This particular shot featured the entire Edwards family; it had been taken by a professional photographer last year. Methodically he traced several of the images, thinking how important each person was to him.

Adoption. Jeremy was of the mind that if Monica were comfortable with that idea, she would have floated it by now. Adoption, an obvious means to the end of having, and raising, a family, had never been mentioned.

So, the biggest question looming involved his own ability, or inability, to reconcile himself to the possibility of being a family of two—him, and Monica.

He had witnessed Monica with children both at her daycare center, and at the dance classes. Now, he felt nothing but a yearning that bordered on jealousy. Over time, she would be able to dote on children. Knowing her condition, she had wisely made them fundamental to her life. She could pour loving energy into their care. How was he supposed to make that adjustment, and find fulfillment? This was all so new to him still, and such a surprising—unexpected—twist of heart.

He paid particular attention to the images of his nieces and nephews. He had always enjoyed spoiling them. If his relationship with Monica continued and grew, his siblings' children would become even more precious; they might help fill the void in his heart.

But it won't be the same.

One by one, different scenarios came to mind: teaching a little boy how to swing a bat, playing catch, helping a little girl color with crayons, or fly high on a swing. He thought of school days, dances, dating and milestone moments like first days of school, driving a car, graduation. Weddings.

Jeremy replaced the picture and rubbed his eyes with a tired sigh. Nieces and nephews were wonderful, but they weren't *his*. He couldn't raise them, or watch them grow each day. He couldn't be the constant they relied upon when they had problems, or when they wanted to share a victory.

But then, like a circle, his thoughts returned to Monica. He couldn't sacrifice his love for her. Not even for children.

I need to adjust, he told himself. *I may have to find a way to be fulfilled without children. And if that's the case, I'll cope somehow. She means that much.*

13

What in the world am I doing here?

Monica sat in a comfortably appointed reception area at Woodland Church. The appealing aroma of fresh-brewed coffee drifted in the air, tempting her to indulge in a cup from the nearby counter-top service. Warm lamplight bathed gently worn wooden end tables that were positioned next to a couch and the easy chair where she sat.

Jeremy *is what you're doing here,* came the annoyingly perceptive reply of her inner voice. *And that should tell you something important.*

She toyed with a couple of magazines that were placed on the coffee table in front of her. *Parenthood.* Oh, sure. *Family Circle.* Naturally. There were even a few copies of *Highlights,* for the kids and a pair of big, colorful Bible books. In nervous repetition, she kept glancing at a closed door bearing a gleaming brass nameplate.

Kenneth Lucerne, Pastor

She gathered a deep breath. It didn't help. She twisted a simple sterling ring round and round her right middle finger.

Girl, you're such a coward! Seriously! This is just a conversation, not an inquisition!

For days after she'd taken Ken's number from Jeremy, she'd studied the small sheet of paper until she knew the sequence by rote, but making the appointment proved to be a challenge. She had picked up the phone—even dialed a couple of times—but promptly hung up before the call connected.

Why did she need God? It's not as though He could change any of the circumstances in her life. Plus, not even a gifted, well-meaning member of the clergy could wave a magic wand and make her infertility go away—or grace her with the children she longed for.

Still, for Jeremy, she had stiffened her resolve and made the jump. After all, what could it hurt?

A click and a soft *whoosh* filled the air. The door to Ken's office came open, and Monica snapped alert, standing up fast. Nerves prickled hot along her arms.

Ken entered the room with a powerful vibration of warmth and a smile that almost set her at ease. "Monica, hi."

"Hi, Ken." She winced. "*Pastor* Ken."

"Ken works for me just fine. Come on in." He gave her extended hand a squeeze when she approached, and gestured to the interior of his office. "Have a seat." He closed the door and crossed to the chair behind his desk. "I'm so glad to see you. Actually, our meeting today aside, I intended to give you a call, unless Kiara already beat me to the punch. We're eager to check out Sunny Horizons. It sounds like a terrific facility."

Monica relaxed. What a nice thing to hear—especially when she considered that Kiara would be a protective first-time mother, and Monica didn't feel like she had made much of a winning first impression on any of the Edwards clan. "Please stop by any time. You don't even need an appointment for a walk-through. My policy is strictly open door. I'd love to show you both around."

"Then we'll do it. Thanks. I admire what you do, Monica. I meant it when I said it's a special gift you share to be so engaged in the lives of children."

Straight away his words cut to the very core of what was taking place in her heart, but he didn't know that, and she needed a few more minutes of assimilation before taking any kind of emotional dive—even with someone as welcoming as Ken Lucerne.

"Let me return the compliment. I enjoyed my introduction to Woodland this past weekend. The services were wonderful."

"I'm happy you were here. Sorry I didn't have a chance to talk to you afterwards. I feel bad about that."

"Don't even worry about it. You were kind of busy." Busy? The man had been corralled by parishioners, and he had focused exclusively on each one. Most of them simply wanted to reach out, extend a hand, an encouraging word, or share a story. A few had talked to him somewhat intently, and he had nodded, held a hand, offered himself as a source of support.

She had enjoyed the ebb and flow of the Sunday gathering, the connection of the people in this faith community. It had felt good to become familiar with the heartbeat of Woodland before attempting this meeting with its pastor.

"I hope we'll be welcoming you again soon." After that, Ken rolled his eyes, and he laughed. "That wasn't about pressure, by the way. Honest."

Monica laughed, and relaxed completely, because he was disarmingly genuine, and sincere. "You don't even need to say the words. No pressure taken at all."

"Good. I'm glad." Ken leaned forward, and settled

his folded hands on top of the desk. "What can I do for you, Monica? What's on your mind today?"

The question was gently framed—curious and nothing more. Still, it stopped her like hitting a brick wall at the speed of Mach 3. Comfort and ease sailed away, replaced by an onset of the trembles. Monica looked into the patient stillness of Ken's eyes and shifted restlessly.

How to begin? Where?

While Ken waited, and gave her space to move forward, Monica could think of only one thing to do. Talk. Come clean. The idea of unburdening suddenly felt right; it would be OK.

Once she reached that decision, the emotional wall burst. "I guess you might say I'm here because I'm angry." She gave a small, sheepish laugh. "Not a very positive way to begin, I suppose, but that hits the worst of it."

"No, Monica. The worst of it isn't that you're angry. The worst of it is whatever creates and feeds that anger. Do you want to talk about that? What's going on?"

Just like that, Ken earned her admiration. This man wouldn't be fooled by coy witticisms. She couldn't help but respect the way he called her out, yet at the same time encouraged her. Ken was easy. Most of all, there was no sense of awkwardness. He seemed not the least bit distressed or dissuaded by her confused attitude.

Like Elise had been. Silence built, and re-fed her tension.

"What happened, Monica?" Ken gently urged.

"I..." She picked up a nearby crystal paperweight. Cube shaped, it was heavy, and prismatic. As she toyed with the piece, its squared ridges and laser cuts captured the desk light and set off rainbows of color. "I had to tell Jeremy that, if our relationship continues, he's going to end up making a sacrifice he never would have banked on."

"What sacrifice is that?"

Monica barely registered the question. She heard the words, but her thoughts spun ahead. Giving them voice became paramount. "It's not something he can control, and it's not even something I can control. It's like this…curse…this inadequacy I've had shoved into my life, and I hate it, and it makes me angry." Her voice rose a bit, and her words, at the end, had begun to rush. She slowed herself. And breathed out.

"What, Monica? What is it?"

The summons was quiet. Monica continued to still herself, muscle by muscle, breath by breath. She looked up at him. "I worry about the fact that the one thing Jeremy probably wants most is something I can't give him. A family."

Ken blinked hard. He opened his mouth, as though to speak, then closed it. He seemed to gather himself. "You can't have children."

"No. No, I can't."

"Oh, Monica—I'm so sorry. Not just for that, but, I can't help thinking about what you must have gone through when Kiara and Daveny announced their pregnancies."

Monica set aside the paperweight with care, and she sighed. "Please don't. On that count, I'm the one who's sorry, Ken. I reacted poorly. I came off seeming rude. I didn't mean to, but that entire day was like enduring a marathon for which I'd never trained." As best she could, she provided him with an overview of that Sunday dinner from her point of view, ending with the fact that at its conclusion, she had informed Jeremy of her condition.

"In so many ways, I lashed out at him afterward, and I know it. The thing is, I didn't know how to stop. Maybe I was testing him, seeing if he'd duck and run. Half hoping he would, maybe. Terrified of what I'd do if he did."

"Why do you think you feel the way you do?"

"Because I'd rather lose him than hurt him." That stilled their conversation for a moment.

"Cut him loose and you *would* hurt him, Monica. Have you considered that?" Ken let her ingest that, regarding her in thoughtful silence. "On the other side of the table, maybe you felt safe enough with him to release yourself a little," he said at length. "Actually, the same thing probably holds true with Elise. You may not know her well, but you recognize her heart, and the love she puts into all of the most important aspects of her life. Especially her children. Those are ties that bind. They're strong and deep. Certainly strong enough to withstand the process of helping someone find their way."

"But she shouldn't have to feel that kind of negativity toward me. I should be a better person than that, and I know it, but I couldn't avoid what I felt. I couldn't make any of the pain disappear, or even diminish. Then, I felt so embarrassed facing Elise again at church."

"Why?"

Monica lifted her hands. "Isn't it obvious?" Ken had been at the family dinner, after all. "I was standoffish, and she saw right through me. Furthermore, I knew my behavior troubled her, but I couldn't seem to draw myself into…into…" Silence fell, oppressive. Hot.

"Into everything you feel you lack, but want more than anything else?"

In reply to those quiet words, Monica nodded and sank against the back of the chair in resignation. "You just nailed it."

"I realize I'm asking the obvious here, something you've probably already given a lot of thought to, but I'm going to ask anyway. What about adoption?"

How could she even begin to express the tumult of emotion that went along with that seemingly innocuous word? All of a sudden, the meeting became difficult again. "I'm afraid of adoption."

"I can't even imagine how intimidating that process would be."

Monica shook her head. "No. I mean, yes. Yes, it's intimidating to go through the process of adoption, but no, that's not the point. Not for me." Silence stretched. "Sure, there's the fear of not meeting the requirements, and of course there's that constant sense of scrutiny and having outsiders dive so deep, and so thoroughly, into your life—past, present and future."

"You get big points for honesty." His praise, his kind smile, drew her gaze to his, and she calmed. But the silence returned. Ken waited for a bit before speaking. "Care to fill me in on the rest of the story?"

"You want to know the truth? It's not very Christian. Part of me knows that, and knows my reasons are wrong, but…"

Ken waited in steady regard, not stepping in. Rather, he watched patiently while Monica felt like squirming. She wasn't proud of what she was about to say, but she'd come this far. She refused to waste the opportunity. "I'm afraid I won't feel the same way about an adopted child that I would for my own, natural child. Isn't that awful?"

"No. It's not so much awful as it is a natural means of questioning yourself. I do think it bears some analysis, though, and prayer time. You don't even need to speak, or perform a litany of needs. Just listen. God speaks in the silence. He'll direct that yearning you feel, and answer all your questions. Just give up this restlessness and clinging to the 'have not.' Let yourself surrender and go still instead. You need to come to terms."

That made sense, but there was a bit more simmering beneath the surface. "The other thing is, I figure why bother? What'll it all come to anyhow? Maybe the message God has been trying to send me throughout the course of my life is that I'm not *meant* to be a mother. Why should I put myself through an additional roller coaster of family issues—with all that anxiety and stress? Know what it's like? It's like I'm just not supposed to have a family, no matter what." She shrugged and looked down, trying to squelch a blooming sense of shame. "It's like I'm not good enough."

"And if you believe that to be the case, I have some advice. Take a long, hard look at how you live your life."

Monica's brows pulled together as she pondered those words.

"Think about what you bring to the children at Sunny Horizons. That's a form of motherhood times the number of students who cross that threshold every single day. Secondly, look at the self-esteem and encouragement you provide those little girls who dance for you every week."

She looked up at him, still puzzling. "But...really? That's just...that's what I do. That's what my life involves." She shrugged. "I made it that way because of emptiness!"

"I don't quite see it that way. I believe you made it that way in answer to a *calling*, Monica. In the life you've been given, you're not just touching two or three or six kids in a blood-linked family. Instead, God's given you a much larger platform. Instead of limiting you, He's expanding the wishes of your heart. Can you can find a way to embrace that fact and stop fighting against what you feel you've been denied?

"It seems to me like you're trying to fit your life into your own set of expectations, rather than taking a different point of view and realizing your prayers have been answered. Look at what you can do beyond being a child's mother by blood. Look at the gifts you give each day, to literally hundreds of kids. Do you think God hasn't heard your longing, and answered it? Not in the square peg to round hole manner you're letting defeat you, but in a broader, more powerful stroke of His brush?"

Jeremy had said much the same thing. Not since her counseling sessions some two years ago had she come so close to confronting the issues, and emotions, involved with infertility. Was God truly at work in this situation? Could she find His hand and hold it fast? "I'm so afraid of botching things up." The admonition came more easily that she'd thought it would. "Jeremy. He means so much to me, and I want to make him as happy as he makes me. I'm afraid of letting him down. I don't want to ruin something that's so good."

"Monica, you've used the word 'afraid' so often

during the course of this conversation. Think about that. You're carrying too much of the weight. Your feelings run deep, understandably. However, I believe the people who care about you will understand and cope with the issues you're facing. Most likely, what they wouldn't be able to handle is you shutting down—or stepping away. Don't be afraid to fight, or rail. Get mad. Release the hurt you feel. But after that? Get square with the life God means for you to live. The blessings you find, I guarantee, will outweigh the losses, if you let yourself move forward into a new perspective. You'll also end up much happier, and in a much better place."

Monica smiled and gave a short, punctuating laugh. "Boy. JB was right about you."

He looked at her in confusion.

"You're good, Ken. You're good at listening, and you're very perceptive."

He dipped his head and shrugged, but she sensed his appreciation.

"When I made this appointment, I didn't believe I'd ever find my way to being open and frank, and comfortable. But I am. Thank you."

His eyes crinkled at the corners just a bit when he smiled at her. "I'll return the favor. Thank you for allowing me your confidence and for letting me get to know you better. What I see happening with you and Jeremy is like watching God unfold a plan, and that affirms my faith. I *always* love that."

The idea of God Himself unfolding a plan that included her and Jeremy, left her feeling humbled, and filled her heart. She stood, and they shook hands across Ken's desk. "I'll be back this Sunday. I'm really looking forward to it."

Ken walked her to the door, which he opened. "That would be great, Monica. I look forward to seeing you."

14

Lunchtime neared, and the door buzzer to Sunny Horizons sounded. From her spot in the pre-K room, Monica heard Deborah greet a visitor, and then she promptly tuned out so she could focus on the kids who stood near. Positioned around a table dotted by oversized papers and paint pallets, about a half-dozen students wore smocks; each wielded a brush to create their own vision of Thanksgiving.

In the week since her meeting with Ken, her optimism crested at a near all-time high. She had seen Jeremy a couple of times since then—for dinner one night, for a chick-flick the next—but only with her sworn promise to view the latest action-adventure movie for their next outing. She had happily conceded the point.

Monica figured it was a point of mutual consent by which, for the time being, they let the topic of infertility rest and focused instead on the process of building their relationship. The memory left her smiling as chatter flowed, and paintbrushes swished earthy, autumn colors across cream-colored paper.

Outside the room, in the lobby of the center, a rapidly escalating conversation drew Monica away from introspection and child play.

"Get out of my way!" a male voice shouted.

That thunderous demand caused the children

around her to go unnaturally still. As one, the assemblage of children turned to Monica in question. Brows furrowed, she walked briskly through the room and yanked opened the door leading to the main room. There she nearly collided with a large, burly man wearing a belligerent expression. Dressed in a business suit, his eyes sparked; his mouth was a tight, hostile line. She closed the door behind her, inserting herself as an added barrier between the man and the children inside. "I'm Monica Kittelski, the director of this facility. Can I help you?" Her words were gracious; her tone wasn't.

"So you're the next one in line? Are you going to try to kick me out, too? I'm Jessica Carter's father. Her *father!* I want to see her. I need to take her home, and as her father, I have the right to—"

Monica pointed to the hallway on her right. "Wait for me in my office and I'll be happy to discuss this matter with you. At the moment, your tone is frightening the children, and I want that to stop." He didn't go down the hall. Instead he moved toward Monica. The hard glint in his eyes and ominous stance made it clear he had every intention of bullying his way inside the toddler room.

"I'm not following you anywhere! And if you don't like my tone, that's too bad! Give. Me. My. Child." He stalked forward until he was right in her face. "Now."

Monica stood firm, arms crossed against her chest. Her eyes didn't waver from his. "Deb, feel free to call the police if he takes another step toward me."

"Gladly, Monica." A quick glance revealed Deb already had her cell phone in hand, ready to dial.

Defeated, but huffing and grumbling beneath his

breath, David Carter turned abruptly and stalked down the hallway.

"I've got your back and I'll stick close." Deb's quiet assurance helped Monica steel herself for battle.

"Thanks."

Monica entered her office with a stride that was deliberately confident. She closed the door, but not completely.

"It's David, correct?" He didn't even reply. Sitting behind her desk, she withdrew the enrollment forms Caroline Dempsey had filled out. For show, she scanned the release authorization form, already knowing what she'd find. "I'm sorry, Mr. Carter, your name isn't on the list of people who are permitted to remove Jessica from my care."

"Take your forms and toss 'em in the garbage, *director*. I want my daughter!"

"Mr. Carter, I don't care who you are. I expect to be treated in a civilized manner." She paused, wanting to add weight to her next words. "I can't turn Jessica over unless you're on this list or I'd be held legally liable."

He cursed vehemently. In a fit of violence, he swiped his arm across Monica's desk, clearing it in one fell swoop. She jumped back and gasped as a pencil holder, files, souvenirs from the kids, all hit the floor in a crashing symphony of sound. The crystal bowl full of jellybeans toppled to the ground as well. Candy bounced along the tile, clattering like keystrokes on a computer until all that was left behind was a heavy, tense silence.

He stalked around the desk; the menacing approach of his tall, somewhat paunchy form was more than enough to prompt Monica to move away and pull her cell phone from the pocket of her blazer.

"Either you give me my kid," he barked, "or I'll take her by force. You have no right to keep me from Jessica!" He toppled her chair, and it collided with the edge of the credenza behind it, causing items stored there to fall and clatter...including her porcelain ballerina.

Stunned, Monica realized she had to move fast, or she'd be the next object of his wrath. She inched toward the safety of the doorway, activating her phone, already punching in a nine, and a one. "Mr. Carter, leave, or I have no choice but to call the police. I've already dialed all but one digit for 911." He gaped at her. His surprise gave her time to open the door. At that point, Deborah practically stumbled across the threshold, her hand on the knob, her cell phone at the ready as well. This, Monica decided, would end promptly. "I said leave. You're disrupting my daycare center, and I want you out of here right now."

"I'll be back," he growled. "Mark my words. Carrie will not walk off with our daughter along with everything else in my life."

Monica didn't even blink. Deborah stood at her side, her eyes narrow, her jaw set. When David Carter left, he slammed the door so hard the windows rattled.

"Deborah, I'm going to call Caroline. Meanwhile, please direct the staff to be alert, and make sure Jessica isn't upset."

"She had early lunch today, so she was outside playing. I'll keep the teachers from talking, and I'll make certain Jessica is unaware of what happened until Caroline can step in."

Monica gave her friend and colleague a wavering smile. Damage control instigated. "Thank you."

"Are you OK?" Deborah finally asked.

"Fine. I just need to take care of my office."

Hot, debilitating rage—*pure* rage—bubbled, rose, then overflowed. The first order of business: pick up the glittering pieces of broken crystal before the kids could get hurt. Monica snatched a broom and dustpan from the nearby storage closet and swept up debris. With a frustrated growl, she heaved the pieces hard, smashing them into the bottom of her steel trash can.

Instant contrition followed, melting her into a puddle of-of nothing.

In physical response, she sank backwards against the side of her desk then slid down slowly, until she was seated, a weakened heap on the floor. She rested her head on her up-drawn knees, barely able to react to the soft crescendo of a nearby whistle that filled the air.

"Nice arm you have there, Jellybean. I had no idea."

Monica shuddered out a sigh. The tips of a pair of slightly worn, brown-leather work boots came into her line of vision, along with the bottom edge of a pair of faded blue jeans.

Jeremy touched her shoulder. "Deb gave me a thumbnail sketch about what happened. It's over, Monica. Come here."

She looked up, silent. He held out a hand, a beseeching look in his eyes. Reluctantly she took hold. She felt damaged. Angry and bitter. Bleak.

Jeremy tugged her to standing. He took the connection a step further and pulled her in snugly, nesting her body against his. Warmth enveloped her. A heartbeat, strong and steady, sounded assurance beneath her cheek. The hard strength of his body became a haven.

"It's OK now."

She dissolved. She rested her head against his chest and breathed deep. The essence of him entered her system in a soothing stream that eased her troubled spirit and settled strong in her heart. His hands rested loose, yet protective, around her. His body aligned perfectly to hers.

That was too dangerous an enticement to a spirit that thirsted for everything he could offer—and everything she *couldn't*. Life was so *unfair!*

Monica stepped away, dropping to her knees to begin scooping up papers, and knick-knacks—like a treasured monkey and elephant combo a class of kids had made for her years ago when they had learned about papier-mâché. Her glance took in the remains of her credenza, and she couldn't help feeling grateful that, though toppled, her porcelain ballerina had survived.

But there were the jellybeans to contend with— currently a rainbow colored booby-trap to the feet that had bounced all over the floor. Tears burned, but she blinked and swallowed, stubbornly refusing delivery. This wasn't her problem, after all; it was David's.

Well, sort of.

Thing was, she was ticked off. In the extreme. So, while she cleaned up, she began to spew and vent, knowing full well that if she didn't, she'd simply burst. "I swear, some people should *not* be allowed the blessing—the flat-out *miracle*—of a child."

"The miracle of a child."

Jeremy's quiet repetition of her declaration caused Monica to pause in the midst of her increasingly frantic organizational frenzy. "Yes," she barked back, stopping just long enough to look into his calm, deep brown eyes. Her arms were now laden by displaced art pieces: a couple of stuffed animals, pictures, a stack of paperwork she'd now have to re-sort. *Oh…!* She dumped the entire stash on the ground; it was too heavy. *Everything* was too heavy for her right now.

She sank into the chair behind her desk, the one JB had righted for her without her even realizing it until now.

"Talk to me." His firm, but gentle demand caused her to exhale a shaky breath; in surrender, she let her head loll back against the comforting, familiar contours of well-worn leather.

"There's nothing to say, JB. Look around you. My office speaks for itself, and Deb gave you the basics. David Carter came in and trashed the place because I wouldn't let him take his child—when he doesn't have permission to do so! The man is a monster. Calculating, manipulative, and he's putting an innocent, unknowing child at the dead center of a divorce target. It's so infuriating to me. Unfathomable. People putting a child into the middle of emotional nastiness—I hate it!"

"And you're allowed. I can't understand his methods, or his actions, either; but I feel your anger at what he's done, Monica."

She went weak. "Please? Call me Jellybean," she whispered sadly.

Jeremy chuckled softly and stepped behind her. He rested his hands on her shoulders and automatically his thumbs pressed into tight, knotted muscles, working them free. His fingertips moved against shoulders held too taut; under his ministrations, Monica felt herself go lax.

Her eyes fluttered closed, and in a second moment

of surrender, she simply let herself rest, content in his care. Until she bounded forward in her chair, eyes wide, remembering herself. "Oh my goodness. Lunch! Leo's Coney Island."

"Which is kind of why I showed up in the first place," he teased lightly. He turned her chair slightly and smiled into her eyes, smoothing a hand against her cheek in assurance.

"Thank God you did."

"Already done."

Monica laughed, turning back and reclining once more. She slid her hands against his. "You're good for me, JB. So good. I only wish I could return the favor." Her words were as serious as could be.

15

It was difficult, but Jeremy forced himself to let Monica's comment rest. Still, for the rest of the day, the residue of it roughed against his spirit like sandpaper. Since their lunch date could only last for an hour, he focused on lightening her mood. He strove to help her work past the dark cloud of confrontation so she could move through the rest of her day at Sunny Horizons.

Before leaving her at the center that afternoon, however, he'd offered to cook dinner for her at her place. And he had a plan brewing. On the way to Monica's that night, he stopped at the local grocery store and paid a visit to the butcher counter.

When she opened her front door a short time later, he offered up a few sacks of groceries, which she accepted with a smile. Jeremy also carried a small package wrapped in heavy, white paper. As he intended, that part of the delivery put a puzzled look on Monica's face. Toby, meanwhile, sniffed and started wagging his tail so hard his entire body shimmied. The dog made low-rolling noises, hopping around their legs when Monica led the way inside. In the kitchen, Jeremy kissed her cheek and chuckled. "I once read that the way to win a woman's heart is through her dog. I'm about to find out if that statement is true."

"Oh, really?"

"Yep."

Monica waited, and watched, while Jeremy unwrapped the package to reveal a large, fresh steak bone. "Can I hand it over?" Even he could hear the hope in his tone.

Judging by Monica's soft eyes and large smile, her heart had indeed been won. "If you don't, he'll probably maul you. Don't let those innocent, velvety brown eyes of his fool you. He's a chocolate lab on the outside, but inside, he's a beast."

"Sure he is." Truthfully, Jeremy couldn't wait to spoil him.

Toby seemed to sense something was afoot, because he whined and bumped up against Monica's body. Then, he changed course and head-butted Jeremy's hand in a playful bid for attention when Jeremy took just a bit too long to surrender the treat. Victorious at last, with the bone clenched in his mouth, Toby trotted into the living room and promptly flopped into place directly in front of the couch. His throaty noises and teeth clicks left Jeremy laughing. "I miss having a dog. I haven't had a dog since I was in high school."

Monica began to unpack dinner supplies. "He's my buddy. I sure do love having him to come home to."

"I'll bet." Jeremy stole another look into the living room. The spot where Toby rested, right next to the coffee table at the left end of the couch, seemed like his natural "spot" in the house. Jeremy could easily picture him in that exact position, right next to Monica's feet, as she curled up each night. Her unconditional companion. She needed that. Her entire spirit yearned for connection. He took in the woman before him. Bursting with spirit and life, it seemed such an injustice that she would never carry a child, and nurture it from conception to birth, and each day of her life thereafter.

He squeezed his eyes shut, shoring up his strength of will. There *were* options. Would she—*could* she—see that?

"You picked up some nice pork chops, JB." Her observation hit him like an alarm buzzer going off. "These'll taste great with a little light breading and some stir-fried veggies, don't you think?"

Jeremy blinked free of his thoughts and found his way into an easy smile. He stroked her shoulder in passing. "Sounds great to me. I figure after we season them up, and put them in the oven, we can take a walk with Toby while they cook." He pulled out some jasmine rice from the paper sack. "We can have this, too."

"Perfect. It's one of my favorites." Her eyes danced with affectionate mischief. "You get Toby a bone, *and* offer up a walk? He's never going to want you to leave."

Jackpot, he thought. Like a conspirator, Jeremy moved close. He nuzzled her cheek, then leaned in. "You've happened upon my ulterior motive," he whispered.

Monica's answering laugh launched his heart.

Minutes later, the meat was cooking, and Jeremy helped Monica slide into her coat. As soon as she jangled Toby's leash, he bounded out of the living room and scrabbled across the tile in the kitchen, meeting them at the back door in a headlong rush.

While Jeremy laughed and grabbed a nearby plastic bag, Monica clipped the leash into place. Toby yipped gleefully while Monica stroked the dog's thick, glossy coat, cooing at him as his exuberance propelled him into hip-hops and dancing circles.

"Toby," she beseeched, "you're going to knock us over! Behave!"

Monica hardly exaggerated. Pinned into a confined space, the three of them were forced to tuck together quite cozily. Jeremy slipped a stray slice of hair beneath the wool cap Monica had just pulled on. "I don't mind." Being pinned against her warm, giving body, even in total innocence, was heaven.

"You don't mind?" Monica sounded a bit breathless. "The six months of traction you'll endure once you tumble down my basement stairs doesn't intimidate you?"

Jeremy just grinned, opening the door so they could leave. Cold air buffeted him immediately, and when he looked over at Monica, he noticed the way her cheeks almost instantly brightened in color.

He laced his fingers through hers, sliding their joined hands into the pocket of his coat. Monica sidled up next to him, leaving no doubt she enjoyed the connection. She stepped that much closer, their steps smooth and syncopated.

A comfortable rhythm in place, a bracing wind at their backs, Jeremy shrugged deep into his coat, and ventured forward. "I want you to do me a favor."

"What would that be?"

"That last comment of yours. At school. Do you remember it?"

Monica drew in the leash just a bit to keep Toby on the sidewalk. She avoided Jeremy's eyes, but she lifted her chin, and he could have sworn she went tight. "Yeah. I remember."

"Well, I want you to explain it to me, because here's the thing: in case you didn't get the memo, you *are* good for me. Why don't you see that?"

Nestled within the thick, wool lining of his coat pocket, her hand went taut in his, so Jeremy stroked her hand with his thumb until the tension eased. Monica finally turned his way and arched a brow, as if waiting on him to draw the obvious conclusion. *Family. Kids.* Inwardly Jeremy sighed, but he drew on his patience, and waited.

Toby sniffed at bushes; he pawed at a few dirt piles and trotted along. His presence, and the motion of walking, lent a calming distraction to the moment. And at last, Monica came forward as well. "It's the story of my life lately. You were actually on my mind all morning, and I felt so good. After talking to Ken, I had a lot to think about, sure, but for the first time I felt *good*. You know, to-the-bone good. I actually allowed myself the luxury of contentment."

"So far, I like where this is headed."

"I did, too. But then, like clockwork, in walked reality. *My* reality. What David Carter did only served to send me crashing down to earth like a meteor."

"Because he has a child, and you don't."

"Not *don't. Never will.* He's been blessed in such a precious way, and doesn't even realize it!" Her frustration bubbled between them like a tangible thing. She picked up after Toby and their walk resumed. "I want to ask you a question."

"OK."

"About adoption."

Jeremy couldn't help looking at her in surprise. Just like that, as prepared as he was to initiate a heart-to-heart conversation about that very topic, Monica came forward on her own. She seemed ready, too, which left Jeremy oddly assured. He slowed his steps, but didn't stop. He tilted his head her way only to find her gaze already latched on him, direct and faultless, sparkling in the overhead light of a street lamp.

"Ask me anything," he said.

"When I met with Ken, he asked me how I felt about adoption. To be honest, and fair, it's not something you and I had a chance to even touch on when I told you about my condition."

"One step, one brick, at a time," he reminded gently.

Monica nodded; her lips even quirked upward a touch, but somberness colored her dimly lit features. Somberness and fear. A sharp ache lanced his heart, a longing to take those two emotions and erase them completely from her heart, and her mind.

"It's a pretty logical, reasonable jump to move from infertility to adoption," Monica said. "When I was diagnosed, adoption was the first thing the doctor talked to me about. He gave me all kinds of advice about adoption as the means to having a family of my own someday, and he encouraged counseling, to get me through the aftershocks of dealing with my condition."

Jeremy nodded, keeping the walk moving slow and steady. He kept his hold tight on her hand as well. "What was your reaction to the idea? Then and now?"

Monica shrugged. "Honestly, back then, the word adoption hit me like a blue fog. It was a word, thrown in among thousands of other words that swirled around me without really sinking in. I couldn't focus on it or anything else, really. The only thing I came away with was the fact that I'd never have children."

"By blood," Jeremy clarified, again keeping his voice deliberately gentle.

Monica sighed. "Yeah, I know. And—adoption is great. I don't have a problem with adoption."

Oh, yes she did. Jeremy heard the word "but" dangling at the end of that sentence as clearly as he felt the first, tentative tingles of snowflakes brushing and melting against his face. "Monica, let me in. Play this thing out so I'll know what you're feeling." *If you don't, we won't stand a chance. I'll have no idea how to reach you.*

The words remained trapped in his throat, but he had the feeling she sensed them anyhow. Her reply confirmed that fact.

"You want the reality, right? Not the candy-coated, public-consumption version."

"Always."

She gave Toby's leash a gentle, guiding tug, turning back toward her house. "Let's go back."

The topic dropped while they prepared dinner, and sat down to eat. Jeremy waited her out, wanting Monica to be the one to take the initiative. They sat across from each other at the dining table in Monica's kitchen; they chatted and relaxed, but toward the end of the meal, Jeremy could only hope his endurance would be vindicated. He craved even a small measure of resolution between them.

"I meant it when I said adoption is great." Monica returned to their critical topic and Jeremy took a deep, relieved breath at her attempt to come forward. "It *is* an answer. For some people. Most people, I suppose. In my case, I'm just not so sure about it."

That statement astounded Jeremy, and this time he couldn't filter, or cushion his words. He got up to pour them both a cup of freshly-brewed coffee. "How can that be? Monica, you'd be perfect."

The surrounding atmosphere featured soft

candlelight coming from tall tapers set in crystal holders at the middle of the table. She had also extended the effort of serving their meal on china of simple, almost translucent white that featured a subtle floral pattern along its edges. The meal was meant to be enticing and intimate.

Now, tension seeped in like an unwelcome blast of cold air. Monica's back went straight. She lifted a linen napkin from her lap and dabbed her mouth. After delivering the coffee, he resettled across from her and longed to reach for her hands. Almost immediately, she had wrapped her fingers snug around the warmth of her mug which rested atop the table for the moment. Slowly, gently he eased them away; that accomplished, he held them firm. Monica swallowed, her eyes downcast.

"Trust me," he whispered. "*Please*, trust me."

Monica's chest rose and fell on a shuddering sigh. "I can't help wondering..."

"About what?"

"About...well...would they truly be mine? Would that bond, that mysterious, irreplaceable bond that happens between a mother and a child, ever come to be? To my way of thinking, that's a connection that can only happen through blood, right? Like your family has. It comes about through the process of carrying an infant from that first second, that first cell burst of creation. A tiny, miraculous being from a communion of body and spirit. From the soul of you and the one you love. That's how I see it, and that's why it means so much to me. I don't see or understand how adoption can come close to that."

She spoke fast, the first sign of letting nerves get the better of her. Jeremy let that truth run its course, and perhaps empty itself into his care.

She seemed unaware of his calm, steady regard. "Then, there's the idea of being given a child to raise through adoption. Well, I can't help thinking…and I cringe at this one because a part of me knows it's irrational and everything else…but what if I get angry at my child, or something goes wrong—an accident, a careless blunder? What about when we make mistakes as parents? What if someone steps in and takes our child away?"

Resigned, out of steam, she slumped her shoulders. She moved a hand from his and lifted her mug, but set it back down without taking a drink. "So, you see? All in all, I'm nothing more than a mixed-up mess about kids."

"Jellybean, you're *emotional* about kids. Big difference. My entrée into your life, then meeting and mixing with my family, hasn't made the issue any easier for you to sort out."

Tears coated her eyes like a shimmering mist. "Jeremy, please don't say that. Meeting you and everything that's come along with it, means so much to me. I'm just—confused. And I'm sorry for that, but it can't be helped. How can I make you happy?"

Heightened emotion tinged her cheeks with red, testimony to the degree of her pain. Now cognizant of how deeply Monica had been scarred, Jeremy watched her with a constricted heart.

He stood and stepped around the table. A glance at her hands told him how tense she had become. Each of her ten fingers had been wound in tight, her rigid posture a fortress raised against attack.

Cautious, Jeremy knelt in front of her chair. He reached up a fingertip and lifted a stray tear away from her cheek. He brought the droplet to his lips and drank it in then cupped her face, all the while transfixed by her turbulent eyes.

He murmured. "Monica Kittelski, you sweet, beautiful woman. What battles you've fought. I don't ever want to negate your feelings. I only wish I could answer the most important questions of all: How come a remarkable woman like you, with so much to offer, can't have children? Why has fate been so unfair? I don't understand it. I never will. The only thing I can do is stand next to you. The only thing I can do is try to reassure you with the love I feel. But I want you to think about something."

"What?" she rasped, looking tired, but she didn't back away, and she maintained their physical, and visual connection.

That lifted his hopes.

"It's true, and unchangeable, that you've been cheated in a big way when it comes to children. But maybe because of that, you've been given the chance to shower love and respect and attention on the kids you work with every day. I've said it before, I know, but you're giving them so much—so many things they need in order to survive. The end result is this: You make a difference. You care. That's motherhood, whether by blood or not."

She studied him for a moment. "Ken said almost exactly the same thing. I heard similar advice in counseling years ago, but JB, something inside me just refuses to absorb it. On one level, I realize that makes no sense, and it chokes off something inside of me, but that's how I feel. I can't get past it. I wish I could!"

Monica blinked fast and hard. She turned away, and he realized at once that she was trying to avoid the emotions cresting over her. Jeremy moved close and took hold of her shoulder. "Stop turning away from me and turn *toward* me instead."

She rested steady and gave him the trust of going still, and listening, despite tears that rolled fat and slow down her cheeks when she faced him once again. "Monica, you have *got* to stop boxing with God."

He maintained eye contact to emphasize his next point. He took hold of her hands, kissing the backs and squeezing them tight. "I don't doubt your stamina, and your strength, but you'll never outlast God, and you certainly can't outrun Him. Look at what's in front of you. Look at your blessings."

Her turbulent eyes delivered the message, as did her silence: she was trying—but with minimal success.

16

In the week that followed, Monica worked hard to make sense of herself.

The dinner date with Jeremy helped her outlook tremendously. It was like he knew her needs clearly; he strived to help her find a sense of equilibrium while her heart spun like a top, bouncing, skittering, bobbling until it rolled into some form of smooth and consistent orbit.

She sought answers just as desperately as Jeremy. That fact alone lent a balm to her stormy soul because it reinforced their mutual depth of feeling. God was moving in her spirit—Ken's council and Jeremy's steadfast support His lightning rod.

Over the next few weekends, she attended church at Woodland with Jeremy and the entire Edwards family. Doing so reinforced a strengthening spirit, and stirred within her a need to do something else—something she hadn't comfortably done in years, almost since her youth.

Pray.

Each night when she first climbed into bed, Monica grew accustomed to the habit of tucking beneath the blankets, clicking off the light, and giving herself over to intensive, from-the-soul prayer sessions with God. Recalling Ken's words helped. No wordy petitions were necessary. Sometimes thoughts and pleas spun through her mind. Other times she simply closed her eyes, sank into her spirit, laid silent and listened.

And she didn't just pray for herself, for answers to the questions she held in her heart. She prayed for her students, and their families—Jessica, Caroline and David in particular. She also prayed for acceptance and a comfortable, more welcoming place within the heart of Jeremy's family—especially with regard to Elise. She even found herself praying, almost automatically, for Woodland Church, Ken Lucerne, and the faith family with whom she became increasingly involved. Woodland possessed a spirit of unity, of loving community that not only drew her in, but became a home to her searching spirit.

Then, into that mystical stillness, worked a song of pure gratitude that left her feeling more centered, and at peace, than she could ever recall. Miraculous voices from the heavens, burning bushes, none of that happened for her; she continued to wonder about where she was meant to go with Jeremy, and how they would handle a mutual desire for family life, but at the same time, she embraced his love, and his every attempt at understanding.

This process of growing taught her patience. Every time doubts set in—every time she felt like her physical emptiness would ultimately let him down—he drew closer, and his intimacy with her spirit only increased. The sessions left her feeling calmer, more receptive and open.

Like God unfolding a plan.

The memory of Ken's words came to her as she drove to Wednesday ballet class with Jessica. She parked her vehicle in front of the community center, smiling at the little girl who rode in the passenger seat. Jessica Carter was fast becoming one of Monica's best dance students. She was committed to learning the dance she'd be performing in the recital a month from now.

"I'll help with your bag, Miss Monica, OK?"

"Sure, Jess. Thank you so much!"

Jessica beamed, flourishing under the positive affection of the adults and kids around her. Today, as usual, Monica allowed for extra time before class started so they could set up, and practice. So, while Monica performed some warm-up stretches, the music for Jessica's performance played and her protégée went to work rehearsing.

Monica watched, and observed, "Your turn was right on the mark, and you ended in first position just like a champ, Jess. You're learning fast."

Jessica relaxed from her graceful pose and bounded toward Monica. "Am I caught up, Miss Monica? I want to be caught up with the other girls. I want to be in the Christmas recital."

"You know as much as they do. You just need to keep practicing. You're very graceful; I'm impressed. The recital will be no problem for you."

Jessica looked at her with happy pride. "I want to dance again, OK?"

"You bet."

Monica reset the CD and pressed play, prepared to coach Jessica's performance once more.

This kind of interaction is what Monica lived for. She was amazed at the little girl's determination. She discovered, during each week's drive to class, that Jessica was a non-stop chatterbox about ballet. Monica had already taught her the five basic ballet positions, and Jessica practiced the steps repeatedly, watching Monica's every move.

For now, Monica gave up stretching and joined her student at the center of the room. They executed the dance piece in tandem with about fifteen minutes left until class formally began.

"Watch your arms," Monica said, pleased when her eager pupil curved them above her head with a beautiful sense of timing and grace. "Good girl! That looks wonderful!" A new part of the recital song began, so Monica continued to prompt Jessica along and perform the routine.

Movement in Monica's peripheral vision drew her attention to the entrance of the room. With quiet footsteps, seeming reluctant to interrupt, in came Caroline Dempsey.

And David Carter.

David fidgeted and shifted. Any semblance of his previous arrogance and hostility was gone. Jessica's back was to the door, but when she caught sight of Monica's expression, she spun, and charged toward her parents. Caroline knelt, and opened her arms to the delighted youngster.

"Did you see me? Did you see me?" Jessica's attention bounced from her mother to her father, her eyes shining and happy. So innocent.

Caroline looked at Monica over the top of Jessica's head. "I'm sorry. We don't mean to interrupt."

Monica couldn't find her voice yet. David Carter gave her a long, unreadable look. He seemed a far sight from the explosive man who had trashed her office, but she had no idea what to expect. He gave Jessica's shoulder a squeeze then crossed the small, open space toward Monica. She fought against the urge to recoil.

But then elements of his approach sunk in—his hesitant footsteps, the apologetic expression on his face. He extended his hand in a tentative gesture. "I owe you a lot more than an apology, but for now that's all I have to give."

Monica felt lightheaded. What was going on here? She accepted David's handshake with a nod, waiting, not knowing what she should say, or do. What on earth had happened?

"I can only explain it to you the way I tried to explain it to Carrie. I was at the end of my rope when I came to your center. I had received the final divorce papers that morning, and everything hit me, and caught up with me all at once. The only thing I could think about was seeing Jessica. All I wanted to do was hold my daughter. Being denied the ability to see her…" The sentence dangled, with no need for elaboration. "Ms. Kittelski, you may not believe me when I say this, but I'm not prone to violence. I never meant for my behavior to–to–well—turn so frightening. You bore the brunt of it, and I'm truly sorry about that. If I can make monetary amends, I will."

Still thoroughly confused, Monica felt a dawning gratitude. Obviously, a momentous shift had taken place within the family relationship that revolved around Jessica. For now, that was more than enough.

"Don't worry about the money," Monica replied quietly. "And as long as you have your focus where it should be, I'm more than happy to accept your apology."

Caroline stepped up, her arm around Jessica's shoulder. "I know the timing is terrible, but we're here because David and I are going to take Jessica out to dinner tonight. He's leaving on a business trip in the morning, or I wouldn't interfere with her ballet schedule. We wanted a bit of time together. You know. As a family." She paused. "Will that be a problem?"

Monica waved that concern aside. "Don't even think about it. As you just saw, Jessica is doing great, and she knows the choreography better than I could hope. Go, and enjoy dinner together."

A few students began trickling in. Before leaving, as David and Jessica left to retrieve Jessica's backpack and ballet duffle, Caroline looked into Monica's eyes with a happy smile. "I'll fill you in when I drop her off in the morning."

Monica couldn't resist giving her arm a squeeze. "Your smile says it all."

"Yeah. I'll bet it does. Thanks for your understanding. You really are one in a million."

A warm flush skimmed upward against her neck and cheeks. "See you tomorrow."

She watched them leave, the two struggling, but hopeful parents with the little girl held between them, their hands linked into a solid unit.

Her heart nearly overflowed with joy—a joy that was tempered only by an acute sense of longing.

ॐঔ

Monica had known Caroline Dempsey less than a few months, but the change in her was remarkable. Reconciliation—coupled with forgiveness—left the woman stronger now; ready to take on the world.

The next morning, Caroline sat in the chair next to Monica's desk at Sunny Horizons, pausing for a few minutes to talk before heading off to work. They shared a cup of coffee, and Caroline began to relay the events that had transpired yesterday. "After what happened at your office, David knew he crossed the line. I was all set to take him down after the way he behaved. I was even ready to threaten him with an outright claim to full custody. Even a restraining order. I was that afraid."

Monica leaned back in her seat, still amazed. "What do you think turned him around? Do you think it was the divorce decree, like he said?"

"I think so." She shrugged. "I didn't even have to make the first move, Monica. We talked on the phone just a few hours after he showed up here—right after you called and told me what happened." They sipped from their mugs; the tantalizing scent of coffee wafted through the air. For some reason, the aroma sent Monica reeling backward, to Woodland, and her meeting with Ken. The earth continued to shift beneath her feet, yet she felt oddly grounded—anchored by…she wanted to say the hand of God.

Caroline continued. "We ended up meeting for dinner at an old-fashioned, mom-and-pop restaurant near where I'm living now. We're not reconciling or anything, but we *are* going to work harder to make sure our divorce remains civil. We have to. After all, we both want to be part of Jessica's life—a *good* part of Jessica's life—and we don't want our problems to become hers."

"Caroline, I only wish everyone were as level-headed."

She shook her head. "Oh, trust me, I have my moments. I mean, I won't be able to trust him completely until he earns it, that's for sure. Still, he apologized. Imagine that! He said he won't interfere with Jessica anymore, because he doesn't want to lose all contact with her."

That was a relief. Monica stood, raising a blind to let in the day's first rays of sunlight while Caroline continued. "I want to believe him, but I'm being careful. I have to, for Jessie's sake."

"I think that's smart."

"I may be going on blind faith, but I've decided to give him the benefit of a doubt. If he breaks his promise, I won't hesitate, so let me know if he bothers you again, Monica. For now, though, I want to try to help him turn a corner. Maybe it'll help smooth out the remnants of our divorce and give us the chance to move on."

"I think it shows a lot of compassion on your part, and some hoped for maturity on his."

"The way I see it, I have to try. We owe Jessica that much."

Faith. Benefit of a doubt.

The words swept through Monica's mind for long moments after Caroline left.

17

He needed to operate from a position of knowledge. At least, that's what Jeremy kept telling himself. Today he was in the office, ostensibly to see to year-end reports, upcoming budgets, and the continuing development of project prospects for the spring season to come.

Today, however, there was more to the story. *Much* more.

Like the two sides of a freshly minted coin, he wanted to explore every possibility, every potential loss—and gain—held deep within the situation he faced with Monica.

Monica. She slid around him, and through him, a cloud of enticement. His brothers' observations at the Lion's game were right on the mark. He was in love. Now, resolving and claiming that fact took priority in his life.

On side one of the coin, Jeremy pictured a family—kids. The vision forced him to analyze the means by which to embrace a life without that link to blood, to tradition and a lasting legacy. On the other side of the coin came a love that would make that sacrifice worthwhile. Monica's verve, her tenderness and playful spirit, engaged him completely.

One side or the other. Heads or tails.

Oddly enough, considering this necessary

reevaluation of his life didn't leave Jeremy with a heavy heart, or a sense of denial. Instead, his mind and heart moved toward resolution; he wanted only to make a way through. He'd swing the hammer, and drive the nail; somehow, a sturdy and comfortable conclusion could be created. For everyone.

He cleared his throat and straightened his back. Rolling his chair close to the desk, he clicked onto the Internet, pulled up a search engine, and typed in three fateful words: *Adoption Agencies Michigan*.

His pulse went erratic. The heat index climbed within the confines of his office. Just beyond the threshold he watched his receptionist, Allison, pass by carrying a stack of file folders in one hand and a lunch sack in the other. She glanced into his office with a warm smile. Jeremy's fingertips twitched on the keyboard. He almost feared she might know what he was doing, and start asking questions, exerting curious, well-meaning pressure. But, of course, that was irrational. She was clueless, yet he was already a wreck.

So this is how it feels, he thought, *when you take that first, fateful step off the edge—the weird quake at the pit of your stomach, the shiver of uncertainty, the hopes, and the fears. This is life-altering huge. Just exploring possibilities feels monumental. How would it feel to be doing this for real?*

The questions and sensations circuited his mind, yet here he was, no more than an outsider looking in. At this point, he wasn't even signing up for anything—he was simply on the hunt for information—processes and procedures—an enlightening degree of background. He wanted to be informed. That's all.

Right?

His conscience, and God's spirit, didn't answer him back right away, so he scrolled, and hummed at some of the agency names he drew his cursor across. *Bethany Christian Services*. That sounded promising. He clicked the hyperlink, and began to wander through the website that opened. The rest of the world promptly faded away.

...Thousands of young women and men choose to make an adoption plan for their unborn children...

...any number of reasons why, but what remains consistent is that they want the very best for their children, and feel adoption can provide it. Bethany has been bringing families together through infant adoption with tremendous success for the better part of a century...

...birth parents relinquish their rights voluntarily, and completely...

...the majority of birth parents meet with the prospective adoptive parents and attain some level of openness in their adoption, even after placement...

That nugget of information caused Jeremy's hand to go still on the mouse. His brows rose. He understood Monica's fears a bit more clearly now, even after just a cursory glance through the information. What if the birth parent, for whatever reason, simply didn't feel a connection with the prospective couple? How crushing would that be, especially since that level of meeting wouldn't come until well into the adoptive process? Still, that degree of openness provided for a commendable and dignified means by which to assure everyone involved. Though difficult in some ways, a pre-adoption meeting with the birth parents made emotional sense, so he found himself in favor of it.

Aside from the potential to be chopped at the knees, that is.

Jeremy climbed deeper and deeper into web-based information gathering, satisfying his questions on one level, opening up all new ones at the same time. He took notes on a nearby legal pad, jotting observations, facts and statistics. After the better part of an hour, he returned to the Bethany site. There he even spent a few minutes watching a video that featured a family telling their adoption story. Intent, Jeremy listened, hanging on every word. There was a happy ending, sure—but what about the times when hopes were dashed? What about the heartbroken birth parents surrendering the life they had helped create? How much strength would that take—to sacrifice a God-given piece of yourself for the opportunity to give a child a better life?

Through it all, Jeremy came back to one fundamental truth: he couldn't blame Monica for being confused, and heart-protective, when it came to an issue that was so important, and, through no one's fault whatsoever, seemed riddled with the chance for heartbreak.

In her case, even *more* heartbreak. All of it centered on family.

Following a heavy sigh, Jeremy stretched, inching his chair backward a few degrees while he pondered. He spun the chair, looking out the window at a line of typically slow-moving lunch-hour traffic. The motion of the cars soothed him almost to the point of hypnosis. And he continued to ponder.

There might even be a third side to this mysterious relationship coin—one he hadn't considered fully until after the football game with Collin and Marty. That third side of the equation included the faces of his nieces and nephews. That particular silver piece encircled his extended family, and the love he felt for them.

But, even with their precious faces in mind, Jeremy couldn't deny the fact that he wanted to know more about the process of adoption. He couldn't help imagining the prospect of welcoming into his heart, and life, the presence of a child who simply couldn't exist in happiness, and security, with its birth parent.

A pair of soft, slender arms slid slowly around his neck, accompanied by the subtle aroma of jasmine and lily. After a bit of a jump he smiled, automatically closing his eyes and going still so he could simply saturate himself with Monica's presence. Her chin came to rest on his shoulder, and she kissed his cheek. "Hi there, handsome," she said softly.

Jeremy took hold of her hands. "Hi there, back." He swiveled his chair around, half-tempted to topple her onto his lap and enjoy a brief, warm snuggle, or perhaps a restrained necking session…

That's when his breath caught. On the screen before him was the adoption site. To his right, a notepad full of information about adoption. In a hurry, but as smoothly as possible, Jeremy flipped over the sheets of paper and clicked the exit toggle to his internet connection.

"Hey, Uncle Jeremy?"

The summons caused Monica to start with visible guilt; she quickly worked free of his grasp. Jeremy stifled a laugh. They were both acting like guilty teenagers. "Yeah, Alex. What's up?"

Ten-year-old Alex Edwards stood before them, carrying a long, cylindrical shipping container. "Mrs. Moynah wanted me to give you this tube. She says the building plans for the Wiltson complex are inside." Apparently nonplussed by Monica's close proximity,

Alex gave her a smile. "Hi, Monica. 'Member me? From dinner?"

Jeremy reclaimed her hand and glanced up at her. "Marty and Steph's oldest," he whispered.

She nodded her recognition. "Absolutely I remember you, Alex. It's great to see you again."

"You, too!"

Monica was dressed in a burgundy wool skirt and a black turtleneck that was cinched at the waist by a thick, black belt. With her patent dress boots, chunky jewelry and upswept hair, she was delicious. Jeremy tore his focus from the lovely blonde at his side and turned to give Alex the benefit of his full attention. "Thanks for the delivery, bud. You can set that on top of the credenza for me."

"Ah, OK. Umm…what's a credenza?" Alex's gaze ping-ponged around the room.

"It's the storage cabinet right behind me."

Jeremy could tell Monica had trouble fighting back laughter at the scene: uncle and nephew, forging a path side by side in the cut-throat, dog-eat-dog world of business and construction.

"I hope you're getting top dollar for your work, Alex," she offered. "I'll bet you've earned it."

The youngster gave her an easy smile. "Oh, I'm here for free. I get to spend the whole day with Uncle Jeremy. It's for school. Isn't that great?"

"It's Take a Kid to Work day," Jeremy elaborated. He handed his nephew a stack of manila folders and a pile of purchase orders. "Alex, there are purchase orders for each one of these job files. Can you match them up for me and paperclip the PO to the top?"

"Sure." Alex looked at Monica. "Uncle Jeremy says we're going to do a power business lunch at—"

Alex checked his wrist watch. "Twelve-thirty. Hey—
that's now. Could Monica come?"

This time she couldn't seem to resist. She burst out
laughing, and gave Jeremy a wicked glare. "A power
business lunch? What are you teaching Alex about life
in the work force?"

"Don't gripe. After all, you're invited. Can you
join us?"

"Frankly I wouldn't miss it. Lunch is why I'm
here. Count me in, gentlemen."

Gratified, Jeremy stood while Alex set the
shipping tube on the credenza.

"Let this be another very important lesson you
learn today, Alex," Jeremy explained with supreme
authority. "The business world is all about establishing
priorities. First, the good stuff. Lunch. Then, the not so
good stuff. Paperwork."

Alex cracked up, and so did Monica. "Got it, Uncle
Jeremy!"

"Nicely done, young man." He looped one arm
around Alex's shoulder, the other around Monica's
waist, and they left the office behind.

18

At the restaurant, Monica watched Alex eat, and she gaped, amazed. "I've never, ever seen a ten-year-old polish off so much spaghetti."

Jeremy laughed. "He's been raised on quality. Outside of a homemade meal, Frank's Trattoria is the best. That's why I brought him here. It's a favorite in our family," he answered between bites of chicken primavera.

Monica shook her head in continuing wonder as Alex soaked up red sauce with a slice of bread, and then devoured it. "Well, he's certainly learning how to put a dent in an expense account." She couched her next question with as casual an air as possible, but deliberately averted her eyes. "So I guess Marty and Stephanie weren't able to take him to work?"

Jeremy shrugged, downing his food with as much enthusiasm and gusto as young Alex. "They could have, but he went to Marty's architectural firm last year. Steph's a residential realtor, and she had a couple high-level property tours, so I told them I'd love a turn."

Monica smiled gently. "I can tell you enjoy it. You're great with him."

Jeremy regarded his nephew with an affectionate look. "I've been looking forward to it, actually. It's fun."

That piece of elaboration was unnecessary. Monica kept her thoughts to herself, but, when she had walked behind Jeremy's desk to announce her arrival, she had seen the webpage left open on his computer monitor and noticed the smooth way he shuffled a stack of papers and a note-filled legal pad. A subtle sense of being "caught" had rippled from Jeremy, but when she didn't make an issue of it, he seemed to relax, and she let the moment pass. She was certain he wanted to keep his explorations a secret. For now, that was fine. After all, Monica faced a similar dilemma. She wasn't at all sure how to respond to her own tumult of emotions about the topic.

Still, avoidance didn't change facts. Family issues built and loomed around them like an oncoming thunderstorm, full of tense expectation, rolling clouds and dangerous, electric undercurrents.

But just like a cloud break, another thought came to mind. As lunch progressed, and she enjoyed their company and interaction, Monica couldn't help but recall her concluding words to Ken Lucerne:

I want to make him as happy as he makes me.

It was just that simple—and just that complicated. Monica toyed with a luncheon portion of lasagna, moving it around on her plate, staring at her food. Sometimes, it felt like getting God to answer a prayer the way she wanted was just this side of impossible. Now, Monica understood why. There was so much more out there, so much love she could hold fast to, if she would open her heart, and her spirit to receive it in faith—and trust.

Watching Jeremy now, realizing the effort he put into ignoring his own call for a family, gave her a lot to think about. He refused to pressure her about her life choices, despite his own depth of feeling. Instead, he attempted to put his nephew at the forefront, exploring the option of becoming even more firmly engrained in the lives of his extended family. His attitude did a miraculous job of tenderizing her spirit, and strengthening the abilities she needed in order to try to move forward in her own way.

Through it all, she became certain of one inescapable fact: she wanted, desperately, to build a life with Jeremy Edwards.

𝄐

Late the next day, one of the teachers opened the door to the rumpus room. "Monica, you have visitors in the lobby."

"Thanks. I'm on my way." She knew she sounded a bit breathless from the exertion of lifting a toddler in both arms and circling him through the room like an airplane. Playtime interrupted, Monica set the boy down and gave him a pat on the back. Walking out of the rumpus room put her directly in the lobby, and when she saw who her visitors were, her footsteps stuttered. Her nerves awakened, and a subtle, anxious tremor began.

Daveny, Kiara, Ken, and Elise turned in unison. They shook snowflakes from their coats and Ken stamped lightly on the rubber entry mat to knock slush from his shoes.

"Hi there!" Monica stepped up in welcome. "Let me take your coats."

"Do you mind the invasion?" Daveny asked, taking in her surroundings with a smile. "Kiara and I had a slow spell at work, and since she's been so eager to see your facility, we figured there was no time like the present to stop by."

"I don't mind at all."

Elise's encompassing sweep of the room struck Monica as sharp, and keen. "This is nice." She pulled off her leather gloves finger by finger. "Still, it's so difficult. Please don't take it personally—I just wish every mother had a chance to be home with their kids."

Monica understood where Elise was coming from. "I know what you mean, but there isn't much of a choice anymore. Even if both parents don't have to work, and one of them stays home with their child, they end up discovering most kids in kindergarten have extensive daycare, or, at minimum, a year or two of pre-school in their background."

"Makes sense. I'm just glad we can come to a center like yours, where we know the owner, and have built-in trust, and respect."

That unexpected piece of praise from Jeremy's mom brought Monica to a stilling pause. "Thank you, Elise. I really appreciate hearing that."

Kiara, who had been wandering, stopped to turn and give them a grin. "She's as protective as any mother would be."

"And I don't blame her at all. Daveny, let me get Jeffrey. He'll be so happy to see you. After that, Ken and Kiara, I'll be happy to show you around."

Moments later, following a stop in the pre-K room, Monica returned, hand in hand with Jeffrey. He let out a happy shout and broke into a run the instant he saw his mother crouch down and open her arms wide in welcome. Daveny and her son settled at a nearby table and began to make good use of the nearby coloring books and a coffee tin full of crayons.

They made the most beautiful picture, Monica thought, fighting back an onslaught of wistfulness that bordered on envy. Two chestnut heads, close together, quietly chatting, filling the pages before them with vibrant colors. Monica closed her eyes, breathed deep, and rebuked the inflow of negativity, focusing instead on the blessing of a tender-hearted mother at play with her child, and nothing more.

After all, a convicting voice inside her said, *what good is envy when you know you could have something just as rewarding. If you let yourself.*

"For now, Ken and I are leaning toward enrolling for childcare once our baby is around six months old or so." Kiara's words ended Monica's bout of introspection.

Ken nodded. "We've both done a lot of figuring, to see how long we can stay home and focus on just being parents."

"After that, I plan on working part-time in the office, part-time at home."

"We can definitely help you out." Monica took the lead from there. " Come on over to the nursery area and I'll show you what we offer." She began their tour at the infant section of her facility where there were cribs, playpens, and a two-to-one teacher-to-baby ratio. There were foam rubber balls, colorful, plastic blocks and a spacious main area with cushioned flooring, and mat games. There were bouncy chairs as well, one of which was occupied by a cooing baby who held hands with the staffer who was seated, cross-legged, nearby. "Also, I can be flexible about scheduling, as long as I have a little notice to plan for staffing."

"Meaning?" Ken had lifted a large, sturdy picture book, but set it aside to focus on Monica.

They continued walking and he kept a protective hand near Kiara's back as she moved forward, taking everything in. Her stomach, Monica now saw, had rounded pleasantly, and a loose-fitting silk blouse flowed around her growing midsection. Monica closed her eyes for a moment, braced against an onslaught of imagined sensations and pleasures: a child's movement within an ever-expanding womb, the roll and thud of a baby's movement. Witnessing pregnancy didn't normally hit her so hard; this time, though, she couldn't escape the alienation she felt. These people comprised Jeremy's world, and occupied his heart. Therefore, all she longed to give him, left her aching.

Discussing Sunny Horizons and focusing on work lent her a needed lifeline. "Well, for example, if meetings come up, where you know you need to shift daycare from one day to another, I can be accommodating. I only need a few days' notice to be sure there's adequate staffing."

Kiara nodded. Her hair was fashioned into an elegant French braid. The style drew emphasis to high cheekbones and creamy skin, leaving wide green eyes the focal point of her features. "That makes sense."

Monica continued to fill in details while they walked. "My infant area is somewhat smaller than the toddler and pre-K program, but we have half a dozen children we care for who are at least six weeks old to eighteen months."

"Hmm." Elise followed them, exploring right along with Kiara and Ken, who conversed quietly, smiling and pointing out items of interest.

Jeremy's mom stepped up to Monica's side. "I see now why Collin speaks so highly of the work you do. Taking care of this many children is quite a challenge.

You have a beautiful facility, Monica."

On nervous automatic, Monica tucked an errant wave of hair behind her ear. She wanted so much to win this woman's good grace and favor. This was Jeremy's mother, a guiding, loving force in his life. Elise was unmistakably sincere, but she searched for assurance as well. She chronicled the most important aspects of Monica's life for two main reasons—the love and protection of her son.

"Thank you very much for the compliment. This center has been wonderful for me. So are the children. I'd miss them terribly if they weren't a part of my life." That comment escaped without a filter. It reached deeper than Monica had truly intended. Elise, however, seemed to bypass the deeper layers. When she laughed lightly, Monica released a relieved breath.

"You'd miss them? Even on snow-bound days like this? They must be hard to handle when they get cabin fever."

Refocused, Monica smiled as well. "True, but you learn to divert and entertain."

"You seem to be a natural."

A drawing of sunshine and rainbows caught her eye; for the time being, Monica turned away from its symbolism. And she opted to leave Elise's comment alone.

Since Ken and Kiara continued to explore, Elise stayed near Monica. "Jeremy tells me you're coming to Becky's wedding in a couple of weeks."

"I accepted his invitation, yes. It sounds like it will be a beautiful event. I haven't been to the west side of Michigan in years, and Jeremy's excited for his cousin, and her fiancé. I'm really looking forward to meeting them."

She was speed talking, and increasingly nervous—and her curiosity was piqued. Why had Elise brought it up? Was she troubled by it? Monica wanted to wince. Instead, she slowed her breathing, and stopped short, wishing she felt more comfortable with Jeremy's mom.

Elise's gaze softened. "Monica, you're trying too hard. Relax. You hold Jeremy's heart, and I know it, so I'll tell you what I've already told him. If that's the case, then you hold my heart as well. And I'm sincere about that."

Monica couldn't find the words she wanted, and needed, to let Elise know how much that statement meant. Her mind spun, but into the vortex came the sound of a loud cry from the next room over. Snapping to, Monica nearly jogged to the rumpus room. There a small group had already gathered around an injured child. "What happened?" She asked the closest teacher.

"Jason and Lindsay were in a bit of a disagreement about who got to play with that big, metal dump truck. They were tussling back and forth with it. When Jason let it go, Lindsay lost her footing and when she fell, the toy truck hit her head."

The teacher made ready to help, but Monica shook her head. "Go ahead and help watch the others. Calm the kids down. I'll take care of Lindsay."

Lindsay continued to cry, hugging her knees to her chest as she rubbed her forehead and rocked back and forth. Monica gathered the little girl onto her lap, holding her close until the tears slowed. There was a small gash on Lindsay's forehead that would require cleaning, some antiseptic and a bandage, but nothing more, thank goodness. She'd be fine.

"You're OK, honey," Monica cooed softly, rubbing Lindsay's back, continuing to cradle her. In silence they rested. Lindsay's sobs lessened to hiccups, and she clung to Monica's neck, her tears warm as they trickled against Monica's skin. Lindsay's breathing eventually evened out, and she closed her eyes with a sigh, just the signs Monica was waiting for. "Let's go back to my office. I'll clean you up and make things good as new. Then, you can come back and play."

"I hate that truck now. I don't want it anymore!"

"For now, I don't blame you, honey, but let's see how you feel once you're back on your feet."

Lindsay sniffled. She looked up at Monica with watery eyes, but an authentic, grateful smile. "M'kay. Thank you, Miss Monica. I'sorry. An' I'sorry to Jason, too."

Monica gave her little student a snuggle. "You're a brave girl, Linds, and I'm proud of you for being sorry about what happened. When we're done, let's have you and Jason apologize to each other. C'mon, sweetie."

They stood and held hands, preparing to move toward the hallway leading to Monica's office. Suddenly she realized she had completely ignored her visitors. All four of them now stood in the rumpus room, watching. In passing, she gave them an apologetic look. "I'm so sorry. I'll be right back."

Ken and Kiara exchanged glances, and knowing smiles. "Actually," Kiara said, "I think we just saw everything we need. Where do we sign up?"

Monica fell victim to a heated flush of shyness and pleasure, but what set her heart soaring even more than Ken and Kiara's show of confidence was the impressed, tender expression presently worn by Elise Edwards.

19

Swags of white netting stretched like curved arms across the length of the ceiling. Clear twinkle lights illuminated the great room of the Baxter Morgan Bed and Breakfast with a creamy glow. Music pumped through the air, sometimes fast and driving, sometimes slow and romantic. The atmosphere was perfect for the wedding reception of Steve Richards and Rebecca Tomblin Richards and the party was in full swing.

Watching the newly married couple dance made Jeremy smile. He held a flute of champagne; best man and maid of honor had just offered their toasts. He stood near the family table, and a pleasing rhythm surrounded him punctuated by chatter, flashbulbs, laughter, music and dishware chiming and clattering as attendees finished eating wedding cake. Swaying a bit, tapping her fingertips on the back of a chair, Monica stood close by, watching the proceedings with a happy look in her eyes.

Jeremy's hand came to rest against the small of her back, and before she could even turn, he wrapped an arm around her waist and tucked in close. She leaned back with a contented sigh, which he could hear despite the party atmosphere. Among many things, he loved her natural, effortless affection, the connected intimacy she created with nothing more than a well-timed caress, or a meaningful look.

At a loss for the moment, Jeremy caught his breath, then leaned in close to her ear. "You seem like a lady who might enjoy a turn on the dance floor."

"You prowling for volunteers, JB?" she teased.

"Actually, I'm quite selective."

The music shifted from fast to slow. Jeremy edged her away from the table. "I'm stealing her for a bit. We're going to dance," he called over his shoulder to his parents and siblings.

She followed his lead, and he ached for the feel of her arms around his neck, the synergy of sharing a tender dance in time to a lush ballad. Jeremy drew her neatly into the circle of his arms. He nuzzled her cheek and Monica slipped her fingertips beneath his hairline, then against the skin of his neck. Jeremy closed his eyes. "Nice."

"Very," she whispered back, settling into the well-executed moves of their dance. She relaxed against him and seemed to drift into the moment, which suited Jeremy just fine. Her natural grace carried him away, lending smooth connection to their movements.

"When the song ends, do you feel like taking a break for air out in the lobby?"

Monica tilted her head to look into his eyes. "Not a minute before, though." They shared a laugh. "Actually, I'd love it. Once I checked into my room and changed for the wedding, I didn't have much time left to explore the place. It seems beautiful."

Jeremy leaned in to skim his lips against her throat. He couldn't get enough of her scent and the satiny texture of her skin. Giving a restrained sigh, he dotted her cheeks with slow, deliberate kisses, nuzzling as they swayed. Monica settled against him; her trusting surrender amplified his determination to remain noble, despite the silken temptation of her lips, the smoke of her deep blue eyes.

Pulling apart at the end of the song left behind an exquisite promise of all that Jeremy knew would come to life between them in the years and decades to come. But that was just it. Life. Life was an issue in need of direct confrontation. He prayed for finesse in what he was about to do, and the guiding stroke of God's hand. God had brought them together. Now, Jeremy relied on Him to keep them together, fulfilled, and united as a couple.

"Let's head to the lobby. There's a sitting area."

Monica fanned her face, shooting him a saucy grin. "Good idea. I'm about to overheat. Maybe because of my date?"

Jeremy loved her playful spark, but longed for seriousness, for open hearts and a bit more vulnerability. So, he held her gaze steady and drew her forward. He detected her answering shiver in the subtle tremble of her fingertips.

"Come here, Jellybean," he beckoned quietly. Enticingly.

Tingles woke up along his skin, transferring, he imagined, directly to her. He turned toward the entrance of the room and led the way through a set of glass double doors. Monica, meanwhile, went shy. The closer they came to the bright lights of the outer reception area, Jeremy noticed her skin's heightened color. She toyed with the slim strap of the evening bag presently secured on her shoulder.

People walked in and out of the entrance of the bed and breakfast, which left the lobby temperature refreshing and cool. Wanting to be attentive, before Monica could even voice the need, Jeremy removed his suit jacket and settled it smoothly across shoulders left bare by a blue satin dress he had admired all evening. He drew her close once the garment was in place.

"Hard to believe there are just a few weeks until the recital," she offered, more timid than he would have expected. That was OK by Jeremy. Being off balance would leave less time for defenses, and those walls she sculpted and nurtured.

"Christmas is coming fast," he agreed.

"You still planning to be there? At the recital?"

"Am I still invited?" he joked.

"Of course." She laughed, a light, happy sound. She seemed to have regained her mental footing. Monica linked her arm through his.

They sat on a couch, in a lobby devoid of crowds. A picture window overlooked Lake Michigan not far beyond; though at the moment, only shore lights interrupted the rich black view. As carefully as possible, he tried to foster intimacy—physical closeness, eye-to-eye connection, linked hands, a light caress.

"This has been a great night," he said softly. Monica's luminous eyes were more than enough to shut off the world around them. No longer did he hear the underlying beat of music from the nearby great room. No longer did he see people floating about, mingling, taking breathers. "And from it, I want you take just one thing, Monica."

She waited, her posture still, anticipatory.

"I'm yours. I'm not going anywhere, no matter what. I have every intention of celebrating a day like this with you. I have every intention of marrying you."

Tears sprang to her eyes. Even though he half-expected them, the evidence of her overwhelmed and tender reaction undid him. "In spite of everything I'm not?"

Those words undid him even further. "Because of everything you *are*. Because of the *love* I feel. I'll deal. *We* will deal. But ask yourself something. From the gut. Are you happy as you are right now? Because if you're happy, I'll be happy."

"I think the answer to that question is pretty clear in the way I live my life. I have enough kids to literally fill a school. The question for me is, will *you* be happy without a family?"

As she waited on his answer, her body went taut. A sharp, squeeze hit his heart when he decided his answer, but really, the choice was no longer his. The decision had been made when he'd fallen in love with her.

"Yes, I will. If I'm being given a chance to spend my life with you, that would be enough to make me happy. Do you want to know why?" Monica nipped at her lower lip and nodded. Jeremy stroked a fingertip against her jaw, trailed it against her throat, then her chin. "Do you remember our kiss? When I saw you home?"

Monica swallowed. "Pretty tough moment to forget."

"You referred to me as chivalrous."

"You are."

"Maybe, yeah. But the reason I walked away that night, the only thing that made it possible for me to back away from you, is the reverence I feel about what we've found together."

"Reverence."

He liked the way she let the word roll off her tongue—slow and savoring. "Yes, reverence. You inspire that deep of an emotion in me. You fulfill and capture a part of me that leaves me in awe. It's a feeling I've never experienced before, and never will again. I'm that certain of you. Of us.

"And whether we were destined to have a dozen kids or none at all, that truth is never, ever going to change." He leaned in and claimed her lips. He coaxed, enticed and captured, drawing her gently forward by a tug against the lapels of his jacket.

"I love you, Monica," he whispered against her mouth. "No matter what. Don't forget that, and don't ever, ever doubt it."

෨ඁ

Monica dealt with the after-effects of a sleepless night, of revelations from Jeremy that knocked her senseless, even now, hours after the fact.

She packed to leave, but her gaze strayed to the nearby window, and its gorgeous view of Lake Michigan. Before heading to church with the rest of the Edwards family, she wanted to indulge one last whim before leaving this gorgeous location. Brisk winter winds or not, she wanted to take a quick walk along the shoreline.

A short time later, she was bundled into a knit cap, thick gloves and a calf-length coat of royal blue wool, traversing the golden beach. Frothy gray water coated the sand, leaving dark marks and indentations as it pushed inland, then receded. Whitecaps rolled forward, ebbing and flowing, as timeless as a heartbeat.

Jeremy's words played through her mind, tempting her to give up her fears, once and for all, in

176

order to cling tightly to a man, and a love, that made her whole for the first time in her life. When Jeremy was nearby, the emptiness in her spirit vanished. Doubts crowding her mind, fled. But when she was alone, the demons seeped into cracks and crevices, where fear and misgiving could bloom large, and flourish.

"Good morning, Monica." She nearly stumbled in surprise at the unexpected greeting.

"Hi, Elise. I see you're willing to brave hypothermia, as well." Monica smiled, but the gesture felt hesitant on her lips.

"I still like Lake Saint Clair the best," Elise remarked. "Although, it's not nearly as impressive." For a few minutes, they walked the beach, buffeted by cold wind, but swept into a majestic view. "Did you enjoy the wedding?"

"Very much."

You know, I have the feeling this might be you and Jeremy before too long."

I'd like to be that lucky, and leave him fulfilled.

"Do you think you could do me a favor?" Elise asked.

"I'll sure try. What's that?"

"Well, we've tap danced around it a bit recently, and the tour of the daycare center ended before I could really speak to you at length...and sort a few things out."

Monica watched Jeremy's mother, encouraging her with a nod.

"I'm hoping you might tell me what lies beneath."

"What lies beneath?" Monica's curiosity built.

"Well, I know we've talked about the day we gathered for dinner, and I've seen how you relate so beautifully, and so openly, to the kids at Sunny Horizons. It's impressive." Elise lifted a shoulder and offered a self-deprecating smile. "I know we've moved past any kind of misconceptions between us, but visiting the center left me wondering what caused it in the first place. If you don't mind my asking, that is…"

Monica sucked in a breath, taken by surprise. There was no acrimony or conviction in Elise's tone, only a request for mutual understanding. Therefore, Monica was completely unsure how to proceed and respond.

Elise gave her a warm, tender smile. "I'm famous for being blunt, so, like I said, please proceed only if you feel comfortable. You're just—you're like a mystery to me. A mystery that involves one of the most precious people in my life, my son."

Monica finally understood Elise's continuing sense of displacement. She didn't know. Jeremy's mom had no idea about Monica's battle with endometriosis. "He never told you, did he?"

"Jeremy?"

Monica nodded in reply.

"Tell me what?"

In an effort to protect their relationship, to guard its development at a very vulnerable, and critical moment, Jeremy had kept her condition a private matter so they might sort out their own feelings and plans before trying to bring family, and all of its attached emotions, into the mix. It was an inherently protective move on Jeremy's part. One that Monica couldn't help admiring. Maybe openness, now, would pave a smoother road for her, and Elise.

"I think it's the answer to those questions you have about me." Chilling winds swept across the water, skimming over the sand, blowing hard through empty tree branches that chattered above them. "I'm unable to have children, Elise. I want them more than anything—but it's just not meant to happen."

Elise stopped walking. Her eyes went wide. "Oh, Monica. That's tragic. Someone with your gifts, and heart? I'm so sorry." Elise reached out and gave her hand a tight squeeze.

"Thank you." Monica didn't know what else to say.

Elise lifted her chin, gathering her poise. "I wish I had known. I certainly would have been more understanding about the issues you faced during dinner that weekend. It must have been awful for you."

"By the same token, I should have been more rational, but it was like a perfect storm coming over me. Please don't worry about it. I'm sorry if I gave you the feeling I don't appreciate all that you did that day—and all that you mean to Jeremy."

"Thank you, but I can't help worrying. Especially about matters that concern my son, and the woman he's fallen in love with."

"How would you feel about that, Elise? If you watched him marry a woman who couldn't have children?"

"I've said it before. If Jeremy's happy, I'll be happy."

Monica quelled the urge to squirm under such a direct and blunt declaration. Instead, she forced herself to relax. "Your family is such a blessing. I envy you their love, and numbers."

"I thank God for each and every one of them, each and every day."

Monica smiled, and nodded. "I would, too. Believe me." Conversation lapsed into the rhythmic, thundering beat of lake waves. "You know, I used to make wild deals with God when I was going through diagnosis. I'd promise him perfection itself if I could only hold a tiny baby in my arms and call it my own, care for it and raise it. To this day I don't think there's much I wouldn't do to have even a cranky, sick child of my own to take care of."

"I can imagine."

"I'd gladly give up a few nights sleep, rush to the doctor or make a midnight run to the pharmacy. I'd willingly sacrifice my time to teach a child to tie their shoes, or ride a two-wheeler. I would have made a good mother. Parenthood is something I'd find hard to take for granted. But then, reality comes crashing in."

"That's where you're wrong." Elise's eyes had reddened, a visible testimony that she shared Monica's pain and sense of injustice. "You could be a fantastic mother, a mother to a very lucky child. Think of what you could do for a child who was born to a woman unable or unwilling to care for it—a child who needs someone like you the most. Is there any better way to become a parent? Blood is blood, but adoption is the means to that same family end as far as I'm concerned, especially for a person like you who has so much love to give."

"I appreciate the support you're giving. I really do, but—"

"No *but*. Don't take the love and needs you feel and push them into remission, or act like they don't exist. That would be a horrible waste of your heart."

"I care about Jeremy so much, but I don't know what to do anymore. We've discussed the issue several times. I give him tremendous credit for being head-on about this. It's awkward, to begin with, and it only gets worse when you know the things you need to discuss are going to make you feel, and seem, less of a woman."

"You feel like you're less of a woman because of infertility?"

Monica nodded. "Without question. I'm less. I'm less than he deserves, less than you'd probably hope for or expect for your son, and beyond that, I can't escape the feeling that, on the whole, I'm just—" Monica shrugged. "Empty."

Their footsteps slowed to a stop. Elise buried her hands in the pockets of her wool coat. For a time she studied Monica, occasionally closing her eyes to take a breath of the water-spiced air. "The only expectation, the only hope, I have for my son is his love and contentment. Whether that brings me twenty grandkids, or none, it's all I care about. You understand that, right?"

"Without question. Your family is beautiful, Elise. I felt...I *feel*...honored to be included as a part of it."

Elise smiled, and moved a few steps forward to link her arm with Monica's. "Thank you. That means a lot."

"I hate that I got off on bad footing with you. And I wish I could be different. For him. I'd love nothing more than to give him the life he envisions."

They resumed walking. Connected. "Well, I'm beginning to understand the battles you've fought. I consider it an honor that you've opened up to me, and I appreciate it. You weren't what I expected, but that's OK. I *get* that now. Revised perceptions and expectations are a blessing." Elise stopped. In posture and gaze, she squared off. "Still, like I said, Monica—there are options."

Options. Everything seemed so simple when placed within the context of that one simple word. Even so, the idea struck like hammer blows against her heart. Monica lifted her face, praying the wind would dry her tears before they fell. "Adoption again."

"Monica, I'm not trying to pressure you, I'm just talking aloud. I haven't gone through the anguish you have, so my perspective is different. So is my objectivity."

The point hit its mark. Monica knew that Jeremy, with his vigor and love, would make an ideal father. How could she have failed to see that fact above everything else? Monica felt selfish, as though she had fallen victim to self-defeating fears.

"Elise, I'm a strong-minded, happy individual."

"We definitely have that in common."

Following a shared smile, they turned back toward the bed and breakfast. "I honestly don't walk around feeling sorry for myself," Monica said. "Doing so is a waste of time. I need to trust God. He led me to Jeremy for a reason. I need to trust that Jeremy and I can work this out together."

"Sounds to me like a wonderful solution, and plan."

"Still, there sure are days, and times, when trouble creeps up on you. Sorry you witnessed mine."

"Understandable emotions, but in real life, you've got to let yourself move on, and embrace a new form of happiness." Elise sighed heavily. "For you, it's the kids. For me, it's watching parades, or any kind of civic military function. To this day, I get such a wicked, burning pain in my heart when I see those gleaming, proud lineups of police officers, or fire fighters, and realize Lance, my firstborn, should have been standing right there among them. With *us*. The badges, the crisp uniforms, the flag. It crushes me sometimes to the point of leaving me out of breath. We should have been given the grace of celebrating Lance's every victory." Elise blinked and swallowed hard. She sighed. "My pain comes from a different source point, but it's powerful; in that respect, I completely understand how you feel. You're right. It can creep up on you out of nowhere. I guess what I'm saying is it's only natural, so forgive yourself and try harder the next time. I know it's the only way I've survived."

Covering her mouth with a shaky hand, Monica looked into the distance, at the ice swept, silver-gray water that stretched to the horizon. Far in the distance, winter birds swooped through the sky, dotting a cloud-banked sky. "How can this whole situation keep such a strong, and terrible hold on my spirit? Ever since I've started going to church with Jeremy, and all of you, I've paid attention to what I've heard, and learned. I fully intend to take what I feel and keep giving it to God, but sometimes it's like He's just not listening."

"He's listening. But He's causing you to grow as well. Growth spurts sometimes cause pain. Maybe He wants you to let go of all the bitterness, and He won't leave the issue alone until you finally do." Elise shrugged. "Collin, went through much the same thing after Lance's murder, so I know the signs."

"It's familiar, and comfortable in its way, even if it's bad. Is that what you mean?"

Elise chuckled wryly. "The devil you know versus embracing the unknown and all of that. Yes."

Monica tucked her fingers beneath Elise's, and, for the first time ever, comfortably held on tight. "I don't want devils. I want angels. I want Jeremy. I want hope, and a future."

Seeming bolstered by their moves forward as well, Elise took hold of both Monica's hands now. She stopped walking, and looked hard into Monica's eyes. "Then I'm going to speak to you like a daughter right now." Her tone was strident. "Don't fear the pathways God gives you. Even if they're not what you might have expected, they'll be full of blessings. And while you're at it, give yourself some breathing room. Pain hits you. Accept it, roll with it, then move past it. When you've been hurting so badly for so long, your perspective can't help but get skewed. Fight back. It seems to me you have more than enough spunk to accomplish that task."

Monica diverted her eyes and her focus; Elise's words turned over and over in her mind. Walking just ahead of Jeremy's mom, Monica picked up a pair of smooth black rocks and tossed them into the turbulent water. "I just don't know where to take things from here. I need to make tough choices. Life-changing choices. I need to figure out whether or not I have the fortitude to move ahead with adoption, or if I can come to terms with the emotional turmoil involved with family, infertility, and the rollercoaster ride of the adoption process. If I don't, I can't lie, or hide from the fact that there's part of me that feels like I should let Jeremy go. He deserves the chance to fall in love again, and have the family he's always dreamed of."

Elise didn't get overly sentimental or verbose. All she said in conclusion was: "I hear what you're saying, and I understand. I just make three requests: First, pray. Pray for discernment—pray for an answer to the doubts you feel. Second, don't underestimate my son."

Silence followed. Monica paused as they entered the bed and breakfast, its warmth a welcome relief from the elements. She turned to Elise. "What's the third request?"

Elise waited a strategic beat before answering. "Don't underestimate *yourself,* either."

20

Sequins, beads and sparkles were everywhere. Nearly a hundred girls between the ages of four and twelve were gathered in the auditorium of Saint Clair Shores High School, dressed in ornate, colorful costumes, preparing for a dress rehearsal of the annual community center dance recital.

Monica assembled her students into one big group and marked attendance for the session. After that, she gave each girl a typed rundown for their parents so they'd know the order they would dance in at tomorrow night's program. Throughout the space, other dance teachers followed a similar routine.

Noise reverberated off the walls, loud but somehow appealing. Oddly, the constant flood of conversation soothed Monica's nerves and kept her from getting swept away by the tense excitement of the girls. Her youngest dancers, Jessica's class, would be the first to go on stage, so she herded them to the wings to prepare them for a run-through.

Petrified, Jessica clung to Monica's hand as she led them to center stage. "Miss Monica, how will I know where to stand? Will you walk us on stage tomorrow?"

"No, Jess. One of the older dancers will. I've assigned someone to lead you on stage. Don't worry."

Monica made her way down the row of dancers and moved them into position for their song. Jessica looked up, seeming determined despite wide, searching eyes. "I'm not scared. Not even a little."

Before returning to the wings, Monica addressed her students. "I'll be right over here, and you'll be able to see me. I'll prompt you along in case you forget a move."

Once the stage lights brightened, about half the girls forgot her instructions and watched overhead with fascination as the technician played with the dimmer, then practiced illuminating the girls with a spotlight.

The music began, and despite the fact that activity in the auditorium came to a stop and everyone started watching them, Monica's students were un-intimidated and performed their dance beautifully.

Afterward, she looked on with a smile as Jessica ran to her mother.

"Mommy! Did you see me? I did it! I did it!"

Wanting to say hello to Caroline, Monica joined them. "Jessica has been so excited that you're getting to see her dance. That's all I've been hearing about at school lately."

Caroline gave her daughter a tight hug. "She did great, but I had the devil's own time trying to get her hair into a bun." She gave Monica a meaningful look then turned to Jessica, "Daddy's going to be here tomorrow night, too, honey. He's excited to see your performance."

That piece of news warmed Monica like a fireplace in wintertime.

"He'll like it, right, Mommy?"

"Absolutely!" Caroline returned her attention to Monica. "You've been so busy! What an event!"

"Actually, I've got a break for the next fifteen

minutes or so while they stage and place a different class. After that, my second group of girls take the stage, and the frenetic pace picks up all over again. I love it, though."

Stage makeup, pink tutu, sequins and all, Jessica plopped herself onto her mom's lap, still squirming and bubbling. "Isn't Miss Monica the *best* teacher, mommy? I love ballet!"

Monica smiled, savoring Jessica's exuberance. "She's a natural, Caroline. I'll bet she inherited that natural grace of hers right from you."

A strange expression glanced Caroline's features. "Oh, I don't think so."

"I take it you're not a dancer."

"Well…ah…" Caroline paused and gave Monica a peculiar look.

Jessica, meanwhile, caught sight of one of her friends and dashed off. Monica watched as the two little ladies compared costumes and ballet slippers amidst chatter and giggles.

"I guess I didn't ever tell you," Caroline said.

"Tell me what?"

"She's adopted."

Monica's breath grabbed, then exited her body in a soft huff of surprise. She hid that reaction well enough, but knew her eyes had gone wide. The revelation about Jessica's adoption was nothing compared to the way this piece of news hit home with her spirit. Monica felt galvanized, compelled forward.

"I'm sorry I didn't tell you," Caroline apologized.

Monica hadn't yet recovered from the surprise, but she managed to say, "There was really no need. I just assumed—"

"That I'm her natural mother." Caroline shifted a

bit, watching after her daughter. Her *adopted* daughter. Monica didn't merely imagine Caroline's soft glow, her maternal—yes *maternal*—pride and connection toward the little girl. That instinct, that love, was real.

This wasn't the time or place, but there were thousands of questions Monica wanted to ask. Was the grueling process fair? Had the uncertainty worn her out? Had the bond between them been easy to forge? Difficult? How old had Jessica been at the time? An infant? Toddler? Had Caroline experienced that gut-wrenching fear about everything falling apart?

Monica, you've used the word "afraid" so often during the course of this conversation. Let it go.

Crystal clear, the memory of Ken's gentle admonishment swept through Monica's mind. And she obeyed his advice. Because ultimately, the only question that mattered had been answered from the start. Love, potent and unbreakable, had brought them together as a family. The love David Carter and Caroline Dempsey felt for their daughter had even helped make a bitter, contentious divorce more manageable.

Excited, determined, Monica considered everything Caroline had been through recently and realized her own fears and misconceptions about being denied a child, and about adoption in particular, weren't nearly as frightening. Caroline had gone to the mat for her daughter; she had fought hard and faced overwhelming adversity. If Caroline could stand up to emotional challenges like that, then Monica felt certain she could give up her own doubts and look more seriously into the prospect of adoption. In affirmation, another memory played through her mind, Elise's concluding bit of advice from when they walked along the lakeshore together:

Pray for discernment—pray for an answer to the doubts you feel.

Monica had. Fervently. Now, Elise's words caused her to realize that getting God to answer a prayer wasn't at all like pulling teeth. It was, instead, a soft, cooling breeze in the dead of a dry, arid summer.

"This may sound crazy," Caroline continued, "but when David and I started having problems a couple years ago, when he became so bitter and angry, I was half afraid the adoption agency would come back for Jessica and take her away—you know, like maybe we were no longer fit parents. Like we were unworthy."

Enrapt, Monica sank onto the velvet-padded theater seat next to Caroline.

"They didn't, of course, but subconsciously, the thought came to me, and rendered more than a few sleepless nights."

Her heart racing, her attention transfixed, Monica nodded. A craving to know more spurred her on. "I don't blame you for your reaction, Caroline. It would have been mine as well. That must have been an awful time for you."

Caroline smiled, an innate gentleness riding along its surface. "It was, but I survived. And so did Jess. Blood ties are blood ties, no question, but Jessica couldn't be more mine—or mean more to me—than if I had given birth to her myself. To be fair, I believe the same thing holds true for David. If not, he wouldn't be so determined about her, and so emotional."

"If you don't mind my asking, what made you decide to adopt?"

Caroline settled back. "We had no luck trying to conceive on our own. We reached that point where we both had enough of the frustration, and decided to go through fertility testing."

A compatriot. Monica wasn't alone. But in truth, hadn't she known that from the very beginning? Between God's love, and Jeremy's presence how could she have ever doubted it? "Do you mind my asking? What did you find out?"

"That the problem was with David." Caroline sighed, and bowed her head. "To this day, I believe that's what changed him. After he found out the test results, I think he started to feel like a failure. Like he was somehow inferior. All of a sudden, he'd go on these awful rampages. He'd blow up at me over the smallest, most inconsequential things. Adoption solved some of our problems, but David was never the same. I tried to stick it out, but our marriage became unlivable."

When you've been hurting so badly for so long, your perspective can't help but get skewed.

Elise's words came back to Monica, hugely amplified. "I can understand that."

"Oh?" Caroline also seemed to realize she had come up against a soft spot.

There wasn't much time left for them to talk. Near the stage, Monica watched her older aged students begin to assemble. Several launched into practicing their arm lifts and plie's. "There's comfort in knowing you've been through upheaval and still kept fighting—not just for you, but for Jessica, too." From there she gave Caroline a thumbnail sketch of her own history.

"Monica, have faith. It's worth it. Take the chance."

Monica watched Caroline in steady contemplation. The fact that Jessica was adopted shouldn't have swayed her so strongly, but somehow it did. Jessica was a wonderful girl, a charmer whom Monica enjoyed teaching and watching over. Jessica proved that there was a lot to be said for adoption, and the emotional threads that ran through it like connecting fibers.

"Thanks." The current performance came from a group of tap dancers who wound down their number. Monica stood to leave so she could organize her next class. "I've got to go, but I'd love to talk more later, OK?"

"Any time, Monica. You've been a God-send to me."

Just like that, with a soul given over to faith, and a heart given over to love, Monica made a resolution. If Caroline could do it, she could, too.

❧

When recital practice finished, she went home and retired promptly to the den. There, she booted up the computer and accessed the Internet. She remembered the name of the site Jeremy had scrawled on the top of his legal pad: Bethany Christian Services. Lots of bullet points had followed, so, Monica figured he had discovered a lot of information and seemed comfortable with the site, and its offerings.

Her body went tense with anticipation; she scratched Toby behind the ears when he trotted into the room and sat primly next to her chair. "Lie down, Tobes," she commanded, ruffling his fur one last time before turning away so she could focus, and jot down some notes of her own.

When she was finished with her discovery session, she moused to the top of the web page, where a toggle directed, "Contact Us."

Monica bit her lip. Restlessly she moved her feet, which caused her leg warmer of a chocolate lab to stir and give a brief, soft whine. She clicked the icon and opened up a new window where she could request additional information. She made a couple of typos because her fingers trembled, but in the end, she sent the e-mail. This wasn't a commitment, after all. This wasn't promising anything to herself, or to Jeremy. This was nothing more than a simple information request.

But that piece of logic didn't quell the images that rolled through Monica's mind. While the transmission zipped through cyber-space, she pictured herself and Jeremy, hand in hand with a dainty little girl, or a precocious little boy, swinging the youngster between them. She smelled autumn, and saw them all jumping into a pile of brightly colored leaves, savoring the family bond of a triple hug.

God's spirit moved through her heart, helping her inch her way forward into foreign, but beautiful terrain.

21

Jeremy focused on the crowd that packed the auditorium. He barely registered the large and pressing body count before he felt a persistent tug on the bottom edge of his suit coat.

"Hi, Mr. Edwards."

He had made his way about mid-way through the theater, searching for Monica, and nearly passed Jessica Carter without a second glance. Dressed in a costume of vibrant pink dotted by sequins, wearing stage-level rouge and lipstick, she was nearly unrecognizable.

"Jessica! Hi!" He grinned, because with her hair slicked back into a glimmering bun, with her peaches-and-cream skin heightened by makeup, she looked just like a porcelain doll. "Wow, look at you. I like your costume."

"Thank you ve'y much." Proudly she brushed at the layers of tulle that formed her tutu. Jessica turned to her mom who sat nearby. "Mommy, this is Mr. Edwards. He's Miss Monica's friend."

They shook hands and Caroline gave him a warm smile. "I remember seeing you briefly at the Community Center. It's nice to meet you officially." Jessica's mother gestured toward a subdued man, dressed in a business suit, who sat next to her. "This is Jessica's father, David."

Jeremy received a tentative nod, and a wavering smile from the man. "I'm glad to meet you."

"Likewise. Enjoy the show."

Space in the auditorium was literally standing room only for the recital, which made it hard for Jeremy to spot Monica in the sea of shifting faces. "She's up front by the stage with the other teachers," Caroline said, seeming to read his mind.

"Thanks." Before leaving though, he cast Caroline a warm glance, and received a friendly nod in return. He squatted, then, to be at eye level with Jessica. Affectionately, he tweaked her chin. "Good luck tonight. I can't wait to see you dance."

She beamed. "OK. Bye!"

When he straightened, he spotted Monica. It never failed to astound him that just looking at her gave him a thrill.

Three rows from the front of the stage, she shared a discussion with parents who sat in aisle seats. She leaned an ear toward them, and laughed. Even from a distance, her smile captivated him. In keeping with this dressed-up event, she wore a knit dress of pale pink that rippled around her legs.

Jeremy moved forward but waited until she was finished talking before gaining her attention. When she turned away from the parents, she caught sight of him immediately. Her smile, intimate and loving, dawned instantly. It made his pulse race.

"Hey!" She stepped into his offered hug. "So what do you think of this chaos?"

"It's...chaos. Seems fun, though." He touched her flush-warmed cheek. "And you're in your glory."

"Well, this glory-girl is on her way to the maintenance office. I've got to see if there are any chairs we can use to set up additional seating in the back."

Jeremy scanned the tight press of bodies. "Is it always this crowded?"

"I've been doing this for five years, and it gets bigger every time." She gave him a rueful look. "Who knows what we'll do next year. We've basically outgrown this space."

He followed her to a set of doors that opened to a school hallway. Dance students gathered there as well as in the auditorium. Excited talk and laughter filled the air, and several girls greeted Monica with happy exclamations.

At the maintenance office door, Monica knocked. A uniformed janitor answered and listened while Monica explained the seating shortage.

"I've got some folding chairs back here. Got some folks who can help carry?"

Jeremy quickly volunteered, and Monica took a few chairs herself, recruiting several fathers of her students along the way. In the theater, the chairs went up, and Monica gave Jeremy a grateful smile. "Thanks for the muscle. Meet me right here when the recital is finished. This is where the parents pick up their kids. Once they clear out, I'm free."

He kissed her cheek and smiled. "See you then. Good luck, Jellybean."

She walked away, but Jeremy had begun to understand her nuances so well that he swore he felt a glow coming from her, a vibration of promise.

"The excitement of performance night," he murmured to himself. "That's what it is."

From a standing position at the rear corner of the facility, Jeremy watched the fruits of Monica's efforts. He paid particular attention to Jessica's class, his gaze straying periodically to the third row, left-of-center position where David and Caroline sat and watched their daughter, united even if no longer married.

Pleasing as that distraction was, Jeremy also kept his eye on Monica. Though nearly hidden by the edge of the curtains, tucked into the wings of the stage, she prompted the dancers along until the song ended, to thunderous applause.

She remained backstage along with the other teachers, barely visible as she watched the progress of the recital. When the event concluded, instructors were called on stage, one by one, and awarded a large bouquet of red roses.

Jeremy's applause rose with that of the crowd, and his heart swelled with pride as she stood in the spotlight for a moment and performed a perfect curtsey.

Afterward, since the hallway became packed with people, Jeremy waited at a side door of the auditorium until he noticed Monica looking for him.

He joined her with a smile. "Pandemonium."

"Yeah. I could meet you outside."

"OK. Want me to take you home?"

People moved past, pressing and pushing as they connected with family members, and recital participants. Monica had one student at her side, tugging on her hand, waiting to offer up a gift bag.

Monica shook her head. "I drove. Tell you what—I have an idea." She bent to whisper a few words to her student, most likely a request for her to stand by for a few seconds. Monica then disengaged from the hubbub around her and stepped up to Jeremy's side. "Give me half an hour?" People moved all around her.

"Yeah."

"Then meet me?" A student stepped up, but Monica's focus stayed put on Jeremy.

"Where?" He felt a heated tingle slide up his arms, through his chest. Foreshadowing of something— something monumental.

She looked him straight in the eyes, and the smile she gave him knocked his senses into a delicious, free-spinning orbit. "At Woodland."

࿐

Jeremy arrived first. He knew the church and its sanctuary would still be open. Wednesday night adult fellowship had ended a short time ago, and Ken generally left the church open for an hour or so afterward. What surprised him was that Monica knew they'd be able to meet here as well.

This really was a blessed place. Woodland was a perfect blend of the old and the new. At first glance, it looked like an old-fashioned country church with aged, red brick, stained-glass windows and white shutters. But behind its soaring, red-brick bell tower and double-door entrance stretched a large, modern sanctuary along with a series of buildings for meetings, staff offices, and the activity center where fellowship took place after each week's service.

Lush, rolling land was framed in by old trees, an ice-laden pond, and a walkway that led to Parishioners Bridge. The wooden structure acted as a memorial to Woodland's members, past and present, with hundreds of names inscribed upon its surface. Just beyond the busy hub of Jefferson Avenue crested the shoreline of Lake Saint Clair, empty and soundless for the winter.

Jeremy loved Woodland deeply. The spirit of this church carried into his spirit like a pulse; it had been that way ever since his youth. The fact that Monica felt a growing connectedness to his faith home lightened him all the more. As he wandered toward the entrance, he noticed Monica's car as she pulled into the parking lot and brought the vehicle to a stop right next to his truck.

He didn't wait. Rather, he entered the sanctuary, claiming a pew not far from the front lip of the altar. So many of the important milestones in his life could be catalogued right here in this spot. Family celebrations of baptisms, service group meetings, weddings, deaths. Jeremy's breath caught when an image of Lance came vividly to life—a deep blue uniform, crisply starched and ironed, bedecked by pins and ribbons; a regulation crew cut; a tight, solid build with wide shoulders and features capped off by a mischievous smile and sparkling eyes.

He dipped his head, closed his eyes and offered it all up to Christ in a grateful prayer.

Lance had been slain by a bullet long ago, yet all these years later, Jeremy still ached at the senseless loss. Although he heard Monica's footfalls along the main aisle, he kept his eyes closed, continuing to pray over Lance's departure, and the hole it left within him. Ironic, he decided, that "The Chief," Collin's little boy who was in part named for Lance, had led him to the woman of his dreams.

❧❦

Monica stood next to the pew where Jeremy sat. She kept a respectful distance, quietly waiting until his eyes came open and he returned to the moment. He turned his head and silently offered his hand.

She promptly accepted the gesture. "You're a million miles away."

"Not anymore."

Monica responded to his saucy reply with a wink. She took him in like the air around her, all spiced by evergreen and bayberry. The energy radiating through her couldn't be denied, or contained. As though it were a talisman, she fingered the large, flat packet she held. She knew full well how deeply its contents could impact them, recognized the world of joyful possibilities its contents could unlock—not just for her, but for the man she loved. Where should she even begin?

"Hi there, by the way," she said at length.

"Back at you. Come here." Using a gentle pull, he drew her onto the pew. "What do you have there? He nodded toward the envelope but Monica placed on the seat beside her. Upside down. For now, protecting its mystery suited her just fine.

She moved close and held Jeremy tight, kissing his cheek slowly. She ignored his question. "Thank you for tonight. For being there for me. I loved seeing you in the audience."

Jeremy nodded, but he kept keying in on the envelope, obviously seeking enlightenment. Monica settled her hand atop the package in an unspoken request that it stay as is for the time being. She leaned back against the pew with a peaceful sigh. "I really do love it here." She studied the empty, echoing space of the church interior. "I should thank you for that as well. For drawing me into a relationship with God, and helping me tune into His truths, and a wonderful church."

"Actually, that's what I was thinking about when you walked up."

Monica tilted her head, her focus centered on Jeremy alone. Her stomach jumped. Tingling sparks ignited her nerves. "Woodland is a place where I can easily make my faith a bigger part of the relationship you and I build together."

Jeremy wound his arm around her shoulders. In his eyes, she saw questions begin to spin and push, but she also noticed the way he set everything aside for the time being. Instead, he kept quiet. Monica, therefore, could unfold as she wished, with no pressure. So, for a time, they simply rested in the serenity of the church. A Christmas tree, toward the right of the altar, was lit by hundreds of tiny, multi-colored lights. A white star graced its topmost branches. The mix of colors from the tree played against the glossy surface of the pew and sparkled in Jeremy's dark eyes. Natural evergreen swags and a pair of matching wreaths dotted the walls; once again she detected the subtle spice of them as she breathed deep—and prepared to open herself in complete love and trust.

"I want to give you an early Christmas present," Monica finally said. She handed him the package, and waited.

Jeremy opened it eagerly, still not seeing the front. From inside he withdrew a thick brochure from Bethany Christian Services along with some printed pages from their website and a few sheets of paper from a notepad which were full of Monica's notes.

His breath caught. He looked at her and she ran her tongue against her lips, watching him right back in a hesitant sense of uncertainty. It was their moment of truth. All that the future might hold, all of her most heartfelt dreams, were about to be confronted. For an instant, doubts tried to ensnare her. Was she being too presumptuous? Had she pushed forward too far? Would he be happy?

"So what you're saying is—" Jeremy didn't complete the sentence. He cleared his throat roughly and blinked hard. When he closed his eyes and took a deep, shaky breath, Monica's every fear, every emotional blockade, and every doubt, evaporated.

"What I'm saying is this: I contacted Bethany Christian Services. I sent them an e-mail, but after work yesterday, I couldn't wait for the information. I made a phone call and asked if I could pick up an information packet in person." Her pulse went wild. Hope set the beat and love flooded her entire universe.

"Before you and I take another step forward," she continued, "before we decide on a future together, and what it can hold, I want you to know something very important." Monica turned to him fully, taking hold of his hands. "I love you." Raw emotion lent texture to the words. "I love you, JB, and I refuse—I *absolutely* refuse—to let anything stand in the way of your happiness. Not even *me*."

"But I *am* happy. Monica, I love you."

He released one of her hands so he could cup her face, and frame it gently. She reveled in the warm, work-roughened stroke of his fingertips. She could scarcely believe the miracle that was unfolding. Droplets of tears built on her lashes and fell. They struck the back of Jeremy's hand when he rested it lightly upon her knee. The moisture glittered like diamonds, like snow beneath a full moon.

"You show me every single day, and in every way imaginable, that you love me." Monica choked back the lump in her throat. "You, and Woodland, have helped me realize how precious I am. You've shown me God's love in so many ways." Her chin quivered, and she lifted a shoulder. "I guess that's been part of my problem all along, until now. Until you. I didn't quite believe God cared about me."

Jeremy moved in haste to interrupt, but Monica held him off by raising a hand. "Oh, I believed in Him, definitely, and truly, but He scared me. I looked at Him as a judge and perfect overseer who weighed right and wrong, catalogued every good deed and every bad. God intimidated me. He walked in unapproachable light, and I was content to cower, and never try to experience His grace in a personal way."

Jeremy remained speechless, and expectant. "After all, really, who am I?" Monica said. "I figured, billions of people on this planet have billions of more problems than I do — and are in much greater need of God's attention than the circumstances of my life. I worshiped Him at a distance. I kept Him remote. I just didn't feel worthy."

The admission caused her skin to burn with heightened emotion. She heard Jeremy's breathing go sharp. "*No*, Monica. *Never*. Please know that."

Tenderly she touched his face. "Then in you came. *You*. You were the answer to all those questions I had for God. You've shown me so much, just in the warm, loving way you live your life. I'm not afraid anymore, of being unworthy, or of loving you, or giving you the life I know we both want. God wrote a message on my heart, Jeremy. He wrote peace, and joy and love on my heart, and every letter of that note is carried in your name. You give me so much. Gratitude doesn't begin to scratch the surface. I'm in awe."

More words, more emotions, tumbled through her soul, but all of them tasted woefully inadequate. So, rather than embellish, she locked eyes with him. The love she found there, the love she hoped he saw in return, was all that was necessary anyhow.

Besides, she'd never get a single word past the lump in her throat.

Monica tilted her head, still connected to him by the touch of her fingertips against his face. "I prayed so long and so hard for the things I wanted," she whispered once she composed herself, "most especially for children. You said it yourself, though. I boxed with God until my perspectives became skewed and I almost lost everything that will bring me real happiness. I didn't realize until now—until you—that my prayers had already been answered. That God had already seen into my heart and provided me with everything I dreamed of—and more."

"He did the same thing for me, Monica, the minute I walked into Sunny Horizons and saw you for the first time. Know that…and believe it…because you've changed me forever."

"I do. Now, I do. But before I could let myself consider this"—she nodded at the packet of information Jeremy had placed next to him—"I had to move past everything I held onto about motherhood and open myself up to other options than having a child naturally. And I needed to realize that there's importance and value to what I do every day at work and at the community center."

Silence filled the air once again. They held hands. Monica rested her head against his shoulder and breathed out in a soft, wavering way. They lingered in Woodland's sanctuary. Jeremy held her close, and they talked. They chatted and planned and dreamed. Much later, they were interrupted by the sound of quiet footfalls, then Ken Lucerne's familiar chuckle. "Hey, guys."

Never looking away from Jeremy, Monica blushed and smiled. "Hey, Pastor Ken."

"Time to close it down. Sorry." Wearing a playful grin, he moved to the altar and unplugged the tree lights, dimming the interior lights as well until the church was bathed in nothing more than a milky, pale glow.

"No problem," Jeremy replied, holding hands with Monica as they stood and prepared to leave.

Monica pulled away. When Ken passed by, she caught hold of his arm and pecked his cheek. "Thank you. Thank you *so* much."

While Jeremy watched them in open puzzlement, Ken looked into Monica's eyes and gave her a knowing smile. "My pleasure. Kiara's waiting, though, so I better hit the road." He glanced at Jeremy, then back at Monica. "Y'know, it's like I always say: there's nothing that affirms my faith more than watching God unfold a plan."

They followed Ken outside. After he slid into his car and drove off, Jeremy stood next to Monica, who made ready to step into her vehicle. "What just happened back there? And how did you know Woodland would be open tonight?"

Monica blinked prettily. "Just a hunch is all." She

lifted to her tiptoes and placed a delicate kiss on his chin.

"A hunch and perhaps the authorization of a certain romance-loving pastor who shall remain nameless."

Monica unlocked her car and opened the door. "Oh, feel free to name him. After all, Ken deserves the recognition."

Jeremy gave her a hug before leaving, then launched into a heated, heady kiss that left Monica hungry on so many levels. "He does indeed, Jellybean."

22

Christmas Eve festivities moved into full swing at the home of Elise and Ben Edwards.

The whole gang attended, including Monica's parents, her younger brother and sister. Seeing everyone together left her with just one thought: *my cup runneth over.*

Jeremy had met her family on a number of occasions, but this was the first time they had all gathered in one spot. After spending the day with Monica's family in Hamtramck, a caravan to Saint Clair Shores took place and everyone now settled at the table of Ben and Elise Edwards for Christmas Eve dessert. Monica couldn't help smiling as she considered the idea that today was but a glimpse of holidays to come.

In the dining room, mini cheesecakes of all varieties, ice cream and coffee concluded the day's festivities. Monica helped clear plates afterwards, working in tandem with her mom, and Elise, Stephanie and Liz, to return the dinner table to some semblance of normalcy. It was a warm, laughter-filled time of sharing.

On her final trip through the dividing doors between the dining room and the kitchen, Jeremy stood and stretched casually. "If you all don't mind, I need to borrow Monica for a minute. We'll be right back."

Naturally, sassy comments and cat-calls accompanied. Jeremy chuckled, shrugging off the jocularity with negligence. Monica just rolled her eyes and grinned while Jeremy took hold of her elbow and led the way out of the dining room. They ended up in the now vacant den of the Edwards' home. Jeremy shut the door, causing Monica to arch a brow. "You're going to ruin my reputation, JB."

"Or save it, one of the two. Have a seat." His lips kept twitching, as though he held back a face-splitting grin by nothing more than a supreme act of will.

"Bossy today, aren't you?"

"Be nice, or no present."

In haste, Monica obeyed, perching with exaggerated perfection upon the edge of the couch cushion. She even added a saccharine sweet smile and wide, innocent eyes to the mix.

Jeremy snorted and rolled his eyes. "As if."

"How rude!"

While they laughed, Jeremy reached behind the couch and pulled out a gift bag. But he didn't hand it over right away. Instead, he sat down as well, and then moved in snug. His kiss slid down her throat in a warm, tingling glide that she welcomed and longed for. His slow-moving touch, against her jaw, then her neck, left her miles away from the celebration at hand. "Merry Christmas, Jellybean."

His breath tickled the inside of her ear when he whispered those magical words. Her head lolled to the side, and a breathy sigh escaped from that achy, quivering spot deep inside. She couldn't keep her eyes open. In fact, she barely found the means by which to stay upright. That was fine, though—a strong, steady pair of arms came around her, and held her fast, drawing her safely home to the haven that was Jeremy Blaise Edwards.

She hardly even realized his intent, but, before she knew it, Monica found herself holding that shimmering, red and green Christmas bag that was flooded by tissue paper of silver and gold. It was heavy, too.

Confused, and brought back to reality, she blinked a few times to clear her vision, and her head. "Ah? What?"

Jeremy stroked her cheek with his thumb. "Ah, that would be a Christmas present. From me. To you."

Her heart sparkled, bursting with joy. He was simply off-the-charts adorable. No other way to put it. He watched her eagerly, peeking inside the bag like a kid as she removed the flood of soft, crinkly paper and set it aside.

Monica uncovered a heavy, dark colored box, hallmarked by the Waterford insignia. Her breath caught, and her gaze lifted to his in the span of time it took for her heart to beat. "Ah?"

"You're becoming redundant."

Monica clucked her tongue at his devilish comment and pulled the lid gently from the top of the box. After carefully peeling back a top layer of cushioning, she nearly burst into tears. From within she gently removed a cut-crystal candy dish chock full of jellybeans. Clear, plastic covering held the candy in place, as well as red curling ribbon.

"Jeremy, this is stunning!"

"I figured you might want a replacement."

The ugliness of the whole confrontation with David Carter seemed so long ago. It had been washed away, cleansed by revised thinking, and a whole new lease on life. Monica speared Jeremy with a look, pushing back laughter, and a grin. "If you think I'm putting a piece of Waterford crystal, your first ever Christmas present to me, on my desk at school where anything could happen to it, you're seriously mistaken. This gets a place of honor."

"First off, I'm Irish, so, what else would I get you but Waterford? Furthermore, your desk at Sunny Horizons *is* a place of honor. It's where we met, and it's where your heart lives."

"Not when I'm next to you," she clarified, slowly swayed by his thought process. She settled the crystal piece on her lap, and pulled the ribbon free. Since the colorful candies were simply too good to resist, she peeled back the securing plastic so she could grab a few.

That's when her diving fingertips came upon an item most definitely not made of sugar.

Monica froze, and her heart rate skyrocketed. "Ah?"

Jeremy, it seemed, could do nothing but laugh with delight at her continuing use of the word "Ah," as well as her reaction to what she pulled from the bed of candies. Her hands trembled. Wide-eyed, for real this time, she stared into his face and fell in love all over again.

"Nothing delights me like catching you off-guard, Monica." He spoke the words softly, with such tender affection her heart flew. He brushed his fingers against hers, taking custody of a breathtaking diamond solitaire set in a slim band of yellow gold. "But you have to answer a question before you get to keep it."

Jeremy didn't go down on one knee. He went

down on both, settling into the space before her, looking up into her eyes while he held her hands gently in his. "Monica," he whispered, for their ears, their hearts alone, "would you do me the *indescribable* honor of becoming my wife?"

She wanted to answer back with her usual display of sass and spark, but her tight throat, her overflowing heart and the love Jeremy showed, all combined to leave her perfectly undone.

She knelt next to him, wrapping her arms around his neck, snuggling into him like a perfectly matched puzzle piece clicking into place and finding home. "Will you do me the indescribable honor of becoming my husband as well?"

She leaned back, giving him a saucy grin through misty, tear-filled eyes. He tilted and wiggled the ring like a temptation. It caught the light and split it into millions of colorful pieces. "I think that could be arranged."

"Ah, the sooner, the better, JB."

"Ah, amen to that!"

With that, as their laughter filled the room, Jeremy slipped the ring into place on the third finger of her left hand. It was a perfect fit.

This was a day of celebrating births—the birth of new hope, the birth of a lifetime commitment made in love, and the birth of a Savior who would see them through it all—good times and bad. So, before leaving the privacy of the den and rejoining the family, they remained kneeling. In unspoken synchronicity, they cuddled together, offering up a prayer of thanks and joyful praise for all they had been given, and all that their lives would embrace.

It was a perfect, blessed moment of communion.